A Time For Gunslingers

A Time For Swapping Lead

A Time For Spilling Blood

A Time For

RANGE WAR

THE
GUNSLINGER

BURT ARTHUR

AN AVON BOOK

ANY SIMILARITY OR APPARENT CONNEC-
TION BETWEEN THE CHARACTERS IN THIS
STORY AND ACTUAL PERSONS, WHETHER
ALIVE OR DEAD, IS PURELY COINCIDENTAL

AVON BOOKS
A division of
The Hearst Corporation
959 Eighth Avenue
New York, New York 10019

First Avon Printing, July, 1966

Cover illustration by Mort Engle

Printed in the U.S.A.

CHAPTER ONE

IT was Tuesday afternoon. However, the usual calm and unhurried way of weekday life in a cattle town was missing. The town was as thronged as though it were Saturday night. The air was charged with excitement, a suppressed excitement that manifested itself in the way in which heads turned at the sound of approaching hoofbeats, in the noticeable letdown when it turned out to be just another rancher or puncher, then in the visible emotional pickup when more hoofbeats were heard. Even the tied-up horses along the street reflected the excitement around them. They trampled one another, crowded against each other, and milled about continuously. The stores were deserted. White-aproned storekeepers and townsmen stood about in little groups, talking and turning their heads and craning their necks when they saw someone else look up the street. There were little groups of women, too; housewives with shawls thrown around their shoulders and marketing baskets gripped in their hands, bonneted women from the ranches, dance-hall girls with rouged faces and brilliantly hued, long-fringed scarves flung carelessly over their bare shoulders, and bright-eyed children of every age listening to their conversation.

The open porch of the Western Hotel was the most crowded spot in town. The incoming stage stopped in front of the hotel, for the company that operated the line maintained its offices there. Actually, the offices consisted of a single room, a hall bedroom which served Jake Holloway as his living quarters, business office and storeroom for his spare equipment. Jake was the company: its president, officers, board of directors, general manager and, when the occasion demanded it, a relief driver. Jake was fifty, thick-necked and heavy-jowled and balding. At the moment he was standing on the hotel steps, and the frown on his face was deepening by the minute.

"That Cal Stebbins," he said darkly to no one in particular. "If that stage ain't on time today, I'll skin him alive."

"What time's he due here?" someone asked.

"Three o'clock," someone else answered.

"Hell," a third man said. "It ain't but a quarter of, so he ain't late yet."

Jake made no further comment. He just hitched up his baggy pants and tightened his belt. When he was annoyed, he didn't want to engage in conversation.

From a window on the upper floor of the hotel, a slim, pretty girl with angry eyes looked down into the street.

"Look at them," she said over her shoulder to a white-haired man who sat quietly in the room's only chair. "Look at them. You'd think they were here to attend a picnic."

The white-haired man arose, looked down into the street for a moment. He patted the girl's slender shoulder, gently yet awkwardly, then he turned and went back to his chair.

"Practically everyone of them has accepted a kindness or a favour from Dad some time or other," the girl went on bitterly. "And now, when he needs help, what are they doing about it? They know those despicable Baileys have imported a hired gunman to kill Dad, so they've come to town, all decked out in their finest, to see the show. That's their way of showing their gratitude."

"There ain't much any o' th'm can do anyway," John Whitaker remarked.

The girl wheeled.

"And you, Uncle John! How can you be so calm about this?"

"Somebody's gotta be."

"Somebody, yes . . . but not you! You're Dad's brother. His only brother."

"Look, honey," Whitaker said patiently. "I've told you a dozen times that everything's gonna be all right. Haven't I?"

"Yes, but . . ."

"Far back as you can remember, I've always kept my word to you. Is that right?"

"Yes, Uncle John."

"Then suppose you quit worryin' and leave things to me like I've told you to."

The girl came away from the window. She seated herself on the bed.

"All right, Uncle John," she said. "I'm leaving everything in your hands."

Whitaker smiled. He reached over and patted her hands.

"Good girl," he said. "Now, whatever happens, take

6

my word for it, Janey, everything'll be all right in the end. All you've got to do is stay right here and keep calm, and when it's over we'll go downstairs and we'll all go home."

There was a sudden pounding of hoofs somewhere up the street, and the man and the girl arose as one and went quickly to the window. Everyone in the street was converging upon the hotel, swelling the ranks of those who had already gathered in front of it. Then the stage came hurtling into view. Presently it braked to a screeching stop directly below them. The driver wound the open-ended reins around the hand brake and jumped down and opened the coach door. A man got out.

"Gordon Bailey," the girl said, and she added scornfully, "the miserable coward."

A second man, bigger and bulkier than the first, climbed down.

"Gifford Bailey," the girl said bitterly. Then she said through her gritted teeth, "I hate him!"

A third man emerged from the stage. He poked his head out and looked about him fleetingly before he got out. He was slim and dark and, when he raised his head and smiled into the sea of faces turned toward him, his white teeth flashed. He held his hat in his hand. It was no ordinary hat. It was black, newer and larger than anyone else's in the crowd, and in the wide ribbon band there were multicoloured stones that caught and reflected the sun's rays.

A path opened, and the Baileys and the third man went up the steps to the porch and into the saloon that occupied the lower floor of the hotel. The crowd, buzzing with excitement, swept in behind them. Jane Whitaker was about to turn away from the window, when she saw a man come out of Hanley's General Store directly opposite the hotel. The man was her father. She knew him at once, but she stared at him as though she had never seen him before. She had never thought of him as an old man. She had never known him to be unequal to anything that arose. Now she saw in his manner a hesitancy, a doubtfulness that shocked her. He was an old man, faltering in his appearance and in his movements, and she interpreted it as a reflection of his own realization that he had come face to face with a situation with which he could not cope. It was an admission that only an old man would make. It was as though Jane were getting her first really good

7

look at her father, a revealing look, and what she saw frightened her.

Her fears for him welled up within her.

John Whitaker's hand tightened on her arm. "Steady now," he said.

Her father walked slowly, almost with measured steps, out to the kerb, and he halted there. He opened his coat and pushed it back, and she saw the holster on his hip. Then another man came out of Hanley's, a tall, lean man, a man whom Jane knew she had never seen before. He backed into the doorway and leaned against the door-frame.

He rolled a cigarette with big, tanned hands, and put it between his lips, scratched a match on his pants leg and touched the flame to his cigarette. Leisurely he tossed the scorched matchstick away. Smoke curled lazily upward from his mouth and from the cigarette and mushroomed against the pulled-down brim of his hat. The girl watched him interestedly, and wished he would raise his head so that she might see his face. Then her anxious eyes shuttled back to her father. She saw him stiffen, saw his right hand drop and curl around the butt of his gun, and she knew the dreaded moment had arrived.

She looked straight down. The Bailey gunman had come out of the saloon, and now he was standing on the porch. He was coatless, and he had left his hat behind him, too. He wore a white-silk shirt, open at the throat, with long full sleeves and tightly buttoned cuffs; tight-fitting, tailor-made pants that accentuated his slim figure; and polished black boots. Around his waist was a gun belt, and a brace of low-slung, black-handled guns, the butts of which jutted out of their tied-down holsters just below his finger tips. He came down the steps unhurriedly, crossed the wooden sidewalk to the kerb and stepped down into the gutter. A cold hand gripped Jane and held her fast in its grasp.

The gunman faced her father and gestured and raised his hands, indicating that he would give Jim Whitaker a chance to draw before he went for his own guns.

"Now," she heard John Whitaker say beside her.

For a moment Jane had forgotten that her uncle was there. She glanced at him, then her eyes raced back to her father. She saw the tall man straighten up and throw away his cigarette. He sauntered out to the kerb, shouldering Jim Whitaker out of his way. Her puzzled, widened eyes raced back to the gunman who was now standing in the middle of the street. He seemed to be crouching a bit, with his arms drawn back and his hands opened, the fingers bent crablike, poised just above his gun butts. Suddenly his hands dropped. The tall stranger moved, too. Jane saw his right arm jerk, saw flame spurt from his hand. There was a thunderous, echoing roar of gunfire that hung in the air for a moment. The window in Hanley's store fell in with a shattering crash. Blue smoke swirled around the tall man. It lifted presently, gently, as though it were a filmy veil that an unseen hand was drawing away.

Jane stole a quick look at the gunman. She stared hard. He lay on his face in the gutter with his right arm outflung and his left arm at his side. The muzzle of one gun peeked out from beneath his body; the other lay just beyond the fingers of his lifeless right hand. She wanted to scream, to cry out, to speak, to give vent to her pent-up emotions; she tried desperately to give voice to something, but the only sound that came from her was a gurgling, choking sound.

"That's all," John Whitaker said.

Mechanically Jane moved away from the window. Her uncle turned away with her, watching her. She stopped abruptly, suddenly weak and ill; she faltered and swayed and instinctively put out her hands, seeking something to hold on to. Instantly he reached out for her, caught her around the waist and held her; she clung to him and bowed her head against his shoulder. When she raised her head, he led her to the bed and she sank down in it and lay back and closed her eyes. He bent over her, held her hands in his and watched her anxiously. A minute or two later, when she opened her eyes again and looked up at him, he was relieved.

"All right now?" he asked.

"Yes."

A stray strand of hair slipped down on her cheek; he eyed it and frowned, then he poked it back into place carefully with a big, thick finger, grunted and straightened up again. He backed to the chair and sat down in it and suddenly smiled.

"Everthing turned out just the way I said it would," he said. "Didn't it?"

She didn't answer. She sat up and got to her feet in almost the same movement, and he looked at her with surprise. Mechanically he put out a detaining hand, but she brushed it aside lightly and went to the window and looked down into the street.

A dozen men were standing in an uneven circle around the sprawled-out figure in the gutter. Blood had begun to stain the ground; some of it ran off and began to blend with the dirt, and the crowd stared at it in fascination, watching it trickle off in various directions. More and more men came up and joined those standing about. A handful of women emerged from the various stores and congregated in front of Hanley's; they talked excitedly among themselves, but none of them showed any desire to view the fallen gunman from anywhere closer up than the far sidewalk. Then a small, elderly woman with a shawl thrown over her shoulders and a marketing basket hanging from her wrist appeared, glanced at the other women as she passed them and stepped down into the gutter. She pushed her way through the men, raised her skirts and stepped over the dead man's outflung hand, bent over him and looked hard at him. At last she straightened up, turned and pushed through the circle, plodded back on to the sidewalk and trudged down the street. The other women followed her briefly with their eyes, looked at one another and shook their heads, then they promptly forgot about her and resumed their talking.

Jane's eyes sought the tall man. But there was no sign of him, and she was disappointed. Then, in almost the same instant, she spied him. He was standing at the entrance to the alley that ran alongside Hanley's. He stood there so quietly, so completely alone, disregarding the women who turned their heads and stole quick glances at him. Some of the men in the gutter looked in his direction too, but he did not appear to notice them.

"Dad?" Jane said suddenly, turning to her uncle. "I don't see him."

"Oh, he's around, all right," John Whitaker assured her. "Maybe he's gone to get the buckboard. Soon's you're ready we'll get out o' here."

"I'm ready now."

"Good. Come on then."

They went downstairs. The saloon was fairly well crowded. The men who were standing at the bar turned their heads and looked at John Whitaker and his niece, as did most of the others who weren't drinking but who were simply idling about, watched them make their way through the smoke-filled place, and out to the porch. As the two went down the steps and across the sidewalk, a buckboard with Jim Whitaker handling the reins pulled up at the kerb. He moved a bit to make room for them. John Whitaker helped Jane mount the high step. As she moved close to her father and seated herself next to him, John, grunting, climbed up and squeezed in, too.

"Either this blamed seat's gettin' narrower," he grumbled, "or somebody 'round here is puttin' on a lot o' weight."

He squirmed and grunted and wheezed and burrowed backward into the vacant space on the normally wide seat, but when he drew no response to his grumblings, he settled himself in frowning silence. The buckboard wheeled and swung wide to avoid the men in the street and the body of the gunman. The right front and rear wheels scraped the kerbing on the far side. Jane, turning her head away when they came abreast of the dead body, met the eyes of some of the women. They stared at her stonily.

The buckboard was nearly at the corner when there was a clatter of hoofs behind it. Jane looked back over her shoulder. The horseman was the tall stranger. He overtook them just as they reached the corner, slowed his mount to a canter, pulled into position directly behind them and followed them out of town. Jane stole a quick look at her father, then at her uncle, but both kept their eyes fixed on the road ahead of them. Presently she, too, settled back.

CHAPTER TWO

THE WHITAKERS and the Baileys owned adjoining ranches that were separated from each other by a strong wire fence that caused no dispute, and by a stream that had been the basis of their quarrels for sixteen years. From the very beginning all their disputes had revolved around the stream, with each laying loud and vehement claim to it. While their deeds read alike—with nothing stated in them pertaining to the stream other than that it was to be considered "free water", to be used by both through mutual and satisfactory arrangement with each other—each claimed ownership. Each did everything possible to discourage the other from using it; at first, discouragement took the form of hard looks and veiled mutterings, then threats and curses. As time went on, blows were exchanged, then shots, but the argument still persisted.

It was only when Lute, Gordon Bailey's son, suddenly bridged the gap between boyhood and manhood that the scales began to tip in the Bailey's favour.

Lute was a husky youth, and a good-looking one, too. He had long been aware of Jane Whitaker, just as she was aware of him. That a friendship between the two had never developed was due to their families' dislike for each other, although there were times when the young people seemed to forget that bad feeling existed between their elders and that they were expected to take the same attitude. Upon those few occasions of forgetfulness, they usually met—accidentally, of course—at the stream. There, Lute, sitting on a big rock at the water's edge and dangling his bare feet in the cool water, would happen to look up and find Jane doing the same thing on the opposite side. Sometimes, though, it was Jane who looked up and found that she wasn't alone. Thoughtlessly they would smile at each other, but very promptly one of them would remember that the other was an enemy, and instantly the smile would vanish and an angry glare would be substituted.

One day when Jim Whitaker was watering some of his stock, Giff Bailey appeared at the stream with an equal number of Bailey steers. One of the Whitaker cattle wandered too far astream and wound up on the Bailey side; Giff not only refused to drive the errant steer back to where he belonged, he jerked out his gun and threatened to blow Jim apart if he dared set foot on Bailey property in an attempt to reclaim the hapless creature. Jim didn't answer, he simply started to cross the stream. Giff unlimbered his Colt and fired so close to Jim's head that the latter, convinced that Giff had meant to kill him, dove deep and nearly drowned himself. He managed to get back to the Whitaker side, but he was thoroughly shaken by his experience, and water-logged. The lost steer was never recovered.

Some days later, when Giff was watering another bunch of cattle, a rifle cracked and a bullet tore his hat from his head. Giff promptly took cover and again unlimbered his Colt; when he failed to locate the hidden rifleman, he cursed and emptied his gun into the brush on the Whitaker side. One of his bullets killed a Whitaker steer that was taking its leisure behind the brush. The next day, when Gordon Bailey (who had been riding the fence) stopped at the stream to let his horse drink, he found two Bailey steers floating in the water close to shore. A hasty examination revealed that both were dead, the cause of death, gunshot wounds.

Another time, when Lute was idling, watching a dozen or so Bailey steers cavorting about in the water, one of the steers took it upon himself to see what the other side of the stream was like, floundered across and started up the Whitaker bank. There was a loud, protesting yell, and Jim, rifle in hand, burst out of the brush. He swung his rifle at the steer and the animal shied, swerved and plodded up the bank and lumbered away. Whitaker, bellowing, reversed himself and scrambled after him. Minutes later he returned, rode down the bank dragging the lifeless steer behind him at the end of his rope. Despite the fact that he was unarmed, Lute came plunging across the stream intent upon squaring things with Whitaker. Jim dismounted, threw up his rifle, and Lute, dripping water, sloshed to a stop. Foolishly, Jim began to taunt the youth who suddenly swept the rifle aside, lunged at him and struck him in the face, stunning him. Before Jim could get his wobbly legs under control again, Lute was in the stream and churning water for all he was worth. He was racing up the Bailey bank when Jim's rifle roared. Lute fell on his face and slid down the bank limply.

It happened that Gordon Bailey was riding by and, when he heard the rifle shot, he wheeled and rode quickly to the top of the bank and peered down. . . . A couple of hours later, when Jim Whitaker was loping along the fence looking for break-throughs, a rifle bullet slammed into his shoulder and nearly toppled him off his startled horse. But he managed to hang on; managed, too, to get back to the house before he fainted away. Both Lute and Jim recovered from their wounds, but neither of them forgot how they had acquired them. From then on no male member of either family dared venture down to the water unless he was covered by a ready rifle.

John Whitaker, the most peaceable member of the warring factions, suddenly took the matter of the stream's ownership to court. When he emerged with a verdict in his favour, the Baileys refused to accept the decision as final. Confident that the Baileys would reconsider and certain that they would not dare oppose the law, Jim posted himself behind some brush just to see what they proposed to do. However, despite his confidence, he did not neglect to take his rifle with him. He was taken back when the Bailey stock came swarming down to the stream. Enraged, he emptied his rifle into the steers; those which survived beat a hasty retreat. The Baileys vowed they would get even. Giff, the more hotheaded brother, publicly announced he would have Jim's life, even if he had to hire someone to do the job.

Giff and Jim met in town one night. There was a brief exchange of words, then a flurry of wildly thrown punches; when a couple of townsmen interfered, Giff turned on them and berated them, even though he had been getting the worst of the fighting. He broke away from them and dragged himself off to the livery stable to get his horse. There was a raising of eyebrows when he reappeared shortly and rode northward instead of heading for home. The following day, Cal Stebbins, Jake Holloway's stage driver, reported that he had seen Giff in Walkersville, some forty-odd miles northward, talking with a half-breed named Spanish Joe. The latter's reputation was well known. He was a gunman, a hired killer, and everyone promptly agreed that Giff hadn't been bluffing when he said he would have Jim Whitaker's life.

It was evening when Jane came out of the house for a breath of air before she turned in. She was sauntering along aimlessly when she suddenly became aware of someone perched on the top rail of the corral. She stopped abruptly. She looked hard at the man, turned and went swiftly back to the house. Her father had brought his account books to the kitchen table; he was sitting down to work on them when Janie came bristling in to him.

"Dad," she said. "That man out there . . ."

"Huh?" he asked, raising his eyes to hers. "What man? Oh, y'mean Kirby?"

"Whatever his name is. I thought he'd gone."

"He was all set to go, but I asked him to stay on a while longer."

"Oh," she said. "Why did you ask him to stay?"

Jim Whitaker took off his spectacles, turned them over in his hand.

"Why?" he repeated. "He botherin' you by bein' here?"

"Yes. He does something to me. He makes me feel cold all over, and goose-pimply."

"He doesn't do that to me," Whitaker said quietly. Then he added, " 'Course with me it's different, being that I know I wouldn't be alive tonight if it hadn'ta been for him."

Jane turned on her heel and went upstairs.

She lit the lamp on her bureau and started to draw the blind over the window when her eyes halted on Kirby perched on the corral rail. She watched him for a moment, then she turned out the light, brought a chair to the window and sat down in it. So his name was Kirby. She wondered what his first name was. She tried matching names. Louis Kirby? Robert? She shook her head. Could it be William Kirby? She gave it up after a while. She wondered about him as she watched him, wondered about his family, and wondered where he had come from. How did a man become a hired killer? What a dreadful profession for any man to follow! Of course, Spanish Joe was a hired gunman too, but he was different. Besides, he was dead, so she wasn't concerned with him. How could anyone be so cold, so hard, so inhuman, so completely devoid of feeling, that he could undertake to kill another man, a total stranger at that, for money?

It didn't seem possible, yet Kirby could, and he had. The dead body of Spanish Joe was proof of it. She shook her head again. She arose, drew the blind and made a light in the lamp, undressed and got into her night clothes, picked a book from among the dozen or so that stood on the small table next to the bed. She was motionless for a moment; she turned suddenly and went to the window and stole a quick look at Kirby, retraced her steps and climbed into bed. She read for a while, but what she read made no sense; she put the book down, got out of bed and went to the window. Kirby had climbed down; now he was leaning over the corral gate and looking skyward.

Again she turned out the light; again she seated herself near the window and looked out. She wondered what a man like Kirby thought about, and what kind of life he led. It was probably a lonely, unfriendly life, she decided. Decent people wouldn't associate with a man who killed for a living. Even those who weren't so decent probably shunned him and shied away from him. She wondered if he could possibly have anyone to whom he could turn. Then, suddenly annoyed with herself for giving him so much thought, she groped her way back to bed and went to sleep.

In the morning, when she awoke and raised the blind, bright, warm sunshine flooded the room. She yawned and stretched and peered out. There he was, and again he was sitting on the corral rail. His horse was jogging about in the enclosure; when Kirby whistled, the horse stopped abruptly, wheeled and trotted over to him. Then he rubbed his nose against Kirby's arm.

Jane had just begun to prepare breakfast when her father came into the kitchen.

"Morning, Dad," she said over her shoulder. He came across the room, and she kissed him lightly on the cheek. "Dad, where did that man, that Kirby, sleep last night?"

"In the bunkhouse."

"Oh," she said.

"Why? The thought o' him bein' here still botherin' you?"

"I just wondered," she answered just a bit stiffly. "That's all."

Breakfast was ready when John Whitaker came downstairs. He pinched Jane's cheek, kissed her on the forehead and sat down at the table. He looked at his brother, but Jim avoided his eyes. Jane brought a platter of steaming hot biscuits to the table, followed it with a platter of griddle cakes and bacon.

"H'm," John said. "Don't they look good?"

His brother offered no comment. He ate sparingly, too, and when he was finished, he got up from the table and went out. John turned to Jane.

"What's the matter with your father?" he asked.

"He—he isn't himself this morning, is he?"

"Nope."

They finished eating in silence.

"Oh, what about Kirby?" John asked as he pushed his chair back and got to his feet.

"What about him?"

"I kinda imagine he likes to eat same as we do. Maybe more so this morning, bein' that he didn't have anything to eat last night. Said he wasn't hungry then."

Jane bit her lip.

Her uncle moved around the table slowly, his eyes on her. He stopped shortly.

"Heard you talkin' to your father about Kirby last night," he said. She flushed and lowered her eyes. She

16

studied her fingernails critically, turned her hands over and looked at them. "The fact is, Janey, we've gotta keep Kirby around for our own protection. The Baileys haven't finished with us, y'know."

She raised her head.

"If you'll tell him to come in," she said quietly, "I'll give him his breakfast."

"That's the girl."

Minutes later Kirby came in, hesitantly, with his hat in his hand. He halted just inside the doorway. Jane was setting a place for him at the table.

"Good morning," he said.

"Good morning," she answered, but she did not look up.

There was a moment's silence, a rather awkward silence for him.

"Your uncle told me to come in for my breakfast," he said finally.

"Will you sit here, please?"

"Thank you."

He put down his hat and came across the room and seated himself. Jane served him, then she placed a cup and saucer at his elbow.

"Would you like your coffee now?" she asked.

"If you don't mind."

"I don't mind at all," she said coldly.

When he had finished eating, he pushed his chair back from the table and arose and pushed the chair in again.

"Thank you," he said.

He picked up his hat and went out and closed the door behind him quietly. A minute after he had gone, John Whitaker returned. Jane was clearing away the dishes.

He said, "That Kirby's kinda nice-lookin', y'know?"

"I'm afraid I didn't notice," Jane replied.

John swung a chair away from the table and straddled it.

"Bet every girl in town'll be makin' eyes at him," he said.

Jane stacked some dishes in the sink.

"Really?"

"Oh, sure! Did I tell you he's from Kentucky?"

"Does it matter very much where he's from?"

"No, I suppose not. Oh, yeah, here's somethin' else about him. He was a captain in the army. In the cavalry."

She turned around.

17

"Uncle John. I'm not at all interested in Mister Kirby. You don't mind, do you?"

"Nope," he said calmly. "I just mentioned those things about him in passin', y'might say." He got to his feet and swung the chair around again and pushed it in close to the table. "He's got a nice name. Vance Kirby. Bet he cut quite a figger in his uniform, ridin' at the head of his men."

"Why did they kick him out?"

"They didn't. He resigned."

"Oh!"

"I think it was on account o' some woman."

"He looks the kind."

"Thought you hadn't noticed what he looked like."

"Uncle John, please! I don't want to talk about the man."

"All right, Janey."

He sauntered out of the house.

Later on, when Jane had occasion to go upstairs, she happened to glance out of the window. She saw Kirby come riding out of the corral, saw him lope off eastward. She watched him for a minute or two, until he disappeared from sight. He rode well, easily, and she found herself picturing him in uniform, riding at the head of his troops.

She wondered about the woman who had been the cause of his resigning from the army. She was probably another officer's wife, she decided. He had probably tried to take her from her husband, and a scandal had resulted. His resignation, she concluded, had doubtless been demanded.

"Janey," she heard her father call.

"Coming," she answered.

She was still thinking about Kirby when she went downstairs.

CHAPTER THREE

It was weeks since Jane had last ridden down to the stream. Now she felt an overpowering urge to go there again. She made no mention of it to her father. The moment he left the house, however, she went flying upstairs to her room, changed into dungarees, blouse and leather jacket, started out of the room only to retrace her steps to her mirror for a last minute look at her hair. She fished a bright red ribbon out of her bureau drawer and wound it around her hair, then she went downstairs and out the back door to the barn. She emerged presently astride her own mare, Velvet. She clattered past the tool shed, and Uncle John, who was inside, poked his head out.

"Hi, young un," he called. "And where d'you think you're going?"

"Oh, just for a ride," she answered.

"Better watch y'self."

"I will."

She loped around the corral and headed eastward. Velvet, eager to run, lengthened her stride. She skimmed over the ground. Jane checked her twice, the second time because she had caught sight of a horseman ahead of her and she had no desire to overtake him. Velvet resented it. She snorted and twisted from side to side fighting for her head, but Jane refused to give in to her, and held her down. Then, in an effort to circle around Kirby, who was probably a quarter of a mile ahead of her, she swung the mare northward, settled herself a bit more comfortably in the saddle and eased up on the reins. Velvet bounded away. Her flashing hoofs drummed over the ground. Some fifteen minutes later they skidded to a dust-raising stop a scant six feet from the edge of the bank, then they went down the incline to the water's edge. Velvet took a mouthful of water, raised her head and whinnied. There was an immediate answer from the opposite side of the stream. Jane looked up quickly. Far down the opposite bank was a horse, and sitting on a rock just a few feet beyond the idling animal was Lute Bailey.

"Come on," Jane said, jerking the reins.

But Velvet wanted another drink. Jane was annoyed; her voice showed it, but Velvet disregarded it. She drank slowly, and finally she backed away from the water.

"Home, Velvet," Jane said.

The mare had other ideas. She plodded along the water's edge, stopped briefly when she spied some fresh young grass and nibbled it. Jane raised her eyes. Lute was watching her. When his horse whinnied, Velvet jerked her head up and answered. She turned and started up the bank, but this time Jane stopped her. She backed the mare down and swung herself out of the saddle.

She picked up a pebble and threw it into the water. She tossed in a heavy rock, and it sank with a deep-throated gurgle. She threw half a dozen more pebbles and rocks into the water, then she looked across the stream defiantly.

"Well?" she demanded. "Haven't you anything better to do than just sit there?"

Lute didn't answer. He didn't move.

"Don't you know it's bad manners to stare at a person?" she demanded.

She picked up a rock and hurled it towards the water. It slipped out of her hand and fell just beyond her with a loud splash. Too late she backed away, drenched. Lute laughed.

"Laugh," she said angrily. "I'd expect that of you."

"Still got that gun slinger around?" Lute called.

"What if we have? Is it any of your business?"

"Nope," he answered quite calmly. "Just wondered. That's all."

"You'd better not let him catch you over on this side," she said. "That goes for all you Baileys."

"We don't aim to go where we ain't wanted."

"Goodness," she said, "you're lots smarter than I thought you were."

Lute got up from the rock.

"Understand that gun slinger's quite a lady's man," he said."

"It's only natural for the women to like him," she said with her nose high. "He's very good-looking."

"Better not let those dance-hall girls in town get near him," Lute said. "You'll lose him sure as shootin'."

"Really?" she said.

"Yeah, and you'd better quit stickin' your snoot out like that. You'll get a crick in your neck."

"It's my neck, isn't it?" she asked icily.

He laughed and stepped up to his horse and climbed up astride him. He looked at her again, and she glared at him in return.

"You're kinda cute-lookin' when you get mad," he said. "Too bad you're a Whitaker. Too bad."

She smiled scornfully.

"But it's lots better than being a Bailey," she said.

He wheeled his horse.

"So long, sweetness," he called and rode up the bank. He stopped when he reached the top, twisted around in the saddle. "Y'know somethin'? 'Course it'll give you a laugh, but it's awright with me. The first time I saw you I decided that someday I'd marry you."

"Real-ly?"

"That's a fact," he said gravely. "But I'm doggoned if I'm gonna marry a girl who hangs around with a gun slinger. You better do somethin' about that, or I'm gonna find me another girl. 'Bye."

"Lute!"

He turned again.

"Yeah?" he asked.

"Ride down here again," she said.

"What for?"

She smiled sweetly. "I want to tell you something."

"Go 'head," he said. "I can hear you up here."

She shook her head.

He rode down the bank and pulled up at the water's edge and looked at her.

"Well?" he asked. "What'd you want to tell me?"

"Just this, Lute," she said. "I wouldn't marry you if you were the only man in the world. What do you think of that?"

He shrugged his shoulders.

"Nothing," he answered calmly. "But you'll change your mind. I on'y hope for your sake that it ain't too late then, because you're gonna feel awful bad seein' me married to some other girl."

"Why, you conceited puppy!" she cried.

She whirled around, reached for the saddle horn and pulled herself upon Velvet's back. The mare turned her head and looked at her. Jane lashed her with the loose ends of the reins, and Velvet went scurrying up the bank.

"Janey!"

She pulled Velvet to a stop, twisted around and looked across the stream.

"I'll probably be back here again tomorrow," Lute called. "In case I get tied up with somethin', I'll make it the day after. I want you to know, because I know you're gonna feel mighty low for bein' so nasty t' me, and you'll be wantin' to apologize. So you look for me."

The reins flicked Velvet's sleek neck, and the mare bounded away. Lute laughed again, then he rode up the bank.

There was no sign of Kirby when Jane rode past the

corral and into the barn. When she emerged minutes later, her father came out of the house.

"Have a nice ride?" he asked.

"Oh, the ride was all right," she answered.

"What wasn't?"

"Lute Bailey."

"Oh!"

"Dad, I don't like him. He's just as smug and as nasty-tongued as the others are."

"Where'd you see him?"

"I rode down to the stream," she replied. "He wanted to know if that—if Kirby was still here. Dad, you're going to keep him on for a while, aren't you?"

"For a while, yeah. How long that'll be, I don't know yet."

"He looks quite capable," she said. "I'm sure he could earn his keep."

He looked at her oddly, but she did not notice it.

"We'll let it lay for a while," he said finally. "We'll talk about it some other time. Look, when it comes time for dinner, set a place for him."

"I will, Dad," she said and went into the house.

But Kirby did not return at noon. It was after one when Jim Whitaker came striding into the house.

"Ain't no point in waitin' any longer," he said. "I'm hungry. Kirby'll eat when he gets back."

Dinner was finished, and still Kirby did not appear. Two o'clock came and went, then it was three o'clock, four, four-thirty and finally five o'clock. Jane marched down the path to the barn and peered in.

"Dad," she called. "Uncle John, are you in there?"

There was no reply, nothing but the pawing of hoofs and the swish of Velvet's tail against the wall of her stall.

She went on to the tool shed, opened the door and looked in, but there was no one in there either. She pulled the door shut. She turned quickly and looked up when she heard hoofbeats. Three horsemen came into view, riding abreast. She recognized two of them at once. The man riding between her father and her uncle was slumped forward in his saddle. When he raised his head, she saw that it was Kirby. Her father yelled something as they swerved towards the corral. When she did not move, he cupped his hands around his mouth.

"Janey!" he yelled. "Get some hot water goin'!"

"Oh, all right!"

22

"Get a bed ready, too! Kirby's been shot!"

She started up the path, looked back over her shoulder and saw the three men pull up at the corral gate. The Whitakers dismounted quickly; together they helped Kirby down from his horse. Jane fled up the path to the house. Quickly she filled a pot with water, put it on the stove and struck a match to the burner; then she ran upstairs and into one of the spare rooms, turned down the covers on the bed and fluffed up the pillows. She went to the head of the stairs when she heard the back door open.

"Awright, Kirby," she heard her father say. "You c'n lean on me."

Presently they were coming up the stairs. John Whitaker stepped ahead of them.

"Got a bed open?" he asked, looking up at Jane.

"Yes. In the room at the far end of the hall."

They backed against the wall to permit her father and Kirby to pass. Kirby did not raise his head. There was a deepening smear of blood on his shirt front, and Jane caught her breath. John Whitaker followed the other two men down the hall, went into the room with them, then the door closed behind them.

Jane hurried downstairs, turned up the light under the pot of water. She snatched a towel out of the kitchen cabinet and slung it over her shoulder, hunted around in one of the cabinet drawers until she found a batch of strips of torn white sheeting and put them under her arm, then she lifted the pot of water off the stove and carried it upstairs. John Whitaker came out of the spare room.

"I was just gonna go downstairs f'r them," he said. "Give th'm to me."

He relieved Jane of the pot. She crumpled the towel and the strips of sheeting and shoved them under his arm.

"Is he—badly hurt?" she asked.

"Yeah, pretty bad, I'm afraid."

"Who did it?"

He shook his head.

"Didn't he say?"

"Nope. Just that somebody'd shot him, and that was all. We asked him again later, but he just shook his head as if to say it was his business an' nobody else's. I'd better go inside. He oughta be undressed by now. Look, we won't be wantin' anything much to eat. Coffee more'n anything else. Put some on, will you?"

It was half an hour later when Jim Whitaker came downstairs to the kitchen. He looked drawn and grim.

"How is he, Dad?" Jane asked.

"Can't tell yet. Got a slug through his shoulder, almost in his chest. An inch or two further down an' it woulda been too bad. How's that coffee comin'?"

"It's ready whenever you are."

"I'm gonna put the horses away, then I'll be back."

"Will you have something with the coffee?"

He shook his head.

"He didn't want us to bring him up to the house. Wanted us to leave him in the bunkhouse."

"That would have been cruel!"

" 'Course. He said somethin' about upsetting you an' some more stuff, but we didn't pay any attention to it."

He went to the door, opened it, stopped and looked at her again.

"I wonder which one o' the Baileys did it?" he mused. Then his eyes gleamed. "Y'know what I think? I think it was that Lute!"

CHAPTER FOUR

KIRBY slept the better part of the evening. The Whitaker brothers alternated with each other in their bedside vigil. It was about nine o'clock when Jane went upstairs, tiptoed down the hallway to Kirby's half-opened door and peered in. The window blinds were fully drawn, shutting out the moon and the night breezes. The lamp that usually stood on the bureau facing the bed had been moved to the far end of the room, and the wick had been turned down until only a tiny light gleamed in the glass globe. Shadows filled the corners of the room. Kirby lay still beneath the blankets, a long, motionless figure. Jim Whitaker sat near him, his head bowed and his chin resting on his chest as he dozed. Jane slipped into the room. A floor board creaked beneath her, and Jim's head jerked up.

"S'matter?" he asked in a whisper.

Jane motioned to him, and he got up stiffly and followed her outside.

"There's a pot of fresh coffee on the stove," she told him in a low voice. "I've put a plate of buns on the table to go with the coffee. Uncle John's going to have some. Why don't you join him? I'll sit with Kirby for a while."

"Y'sure you won't mind?"

"Of course not."

"I'll make it quick."

"You needn't hurry. I've nothing else to do, and I don't feel sleepy enough to go to bed."

He nodded, stepped around her and went down the stairs.

Jane seated herself beside the bed. Kirby stirred and sighed. She got up and bent over him and drew the covers a bit higher around him. He moved his head, and her hand brushed his cheek. It was hot. She touched his forehead, shook her head and went quickly out of the room and downstairs to the kitchen. Her father and her uncle looked up from their coffee.

"He's feverish," she said. "I'm going to bathe his face and wrists with water and alcohol."

Neither man said anything. They watched her fill a basin with water, watched her add some alcohol to it. After she had gone upstairs again, Jim Whitaker sat back in his chair.

"'Bout time we got a doctor in this county," he said. "Far as I know there ain't any within sixty miles o' here."

"Closer to seventy," John Whitaker said. "That is, 'less that feller they had in Red River's moved on somewhere's. I haven't heard any mention o' him in a long time, so it might be he's dead."

Using a bit of towelling that had once been part of a full-sized towel, Jane bathed Kirby's flushed face and wrists. At first he threshed about and turned his head away, but after a while he lay still and offered no further resistance. When she was finished, she put the basin on the bureau, felt his face and forehead again; then satisfied that the bathing had soothed him and helped reduce his fever, she sat down again. He stirred shortly. His lips moved and she leaned towards him.

"Diane," she heard him say in a faraway voice. He pushed the covers off. "Diane," he said again.

She drew the covers up around him. His lips looked parched. There was a pitcher of water and a glass on the washstand on the other side of the room. She arose and poured some water into the glass, bent over him and tried to get him to swallow some of it. He turned his head away each time she brought the glass close, and finally she

25

slipped her arm under his head and raised him; then she was able to get a bit of the water into his mouth. Some of it dribbled out of the corner of his mouth and ran down his chin, and she wiped it away gently.

She heard a step and looked around. John Whitaker came into the room.

"How is he?" he asked in a whisper.

"He doesn't seem to be so flushed."

"Good. Now suppose you let me take over?"

Kirby stirred, and they looked at him.

"Diane," he said again, "I tell you it's no use. It wouldn't be fair to him, and it wouldn't work out for us."

Uncle John's eyebrows arched. "What d'you suppose that was all about?" he mused.

"No, Diane," Kirby said. "It wouldn't work out. Can't you see that?"

Uncle John touched Jane's arm, and she looked up at him.

"Why don't you turn in?" he asked. "You must be tired now."

"In a little while," she replied.

John Whitaker didn't press the point; he went around to the other side of the bed.

"Diane," Kirby said again, "he's my friend. My best friend. He saved my life once. I can't do this to him. You mustn't ask me to."

Uncle John came back to Jane's side.

"Wonder if that's the woman who . . ."

"Sh-h!" Jane said.

But Kirby was silent now. He seemed to burrow deeper into the bedding. When Jane half arose and touched his cheek, Uncle John looked at her questioningly. She raised her eyes to his and smiled her answer. She smoothed the bed covers, then she got up.

"I'm going into my room," she whispered to her uncle. "I'm going to read for a while. If you want me for anything please call me."

He nodded.

"Is Dad downstairs?"

"Yes. Just sittin' there."

"I'll go downstairs for a moment and say good night to him."

The bright sunshine streaming into her room awoke Jane the next morning. She overcame an urge to sleep a bit longer, got out of bed and went to the window in her bare feet and looked out. It was a glorious morning. The blind, she discovered, had run up on the roller. She raised the window, and the curtains billowed in the surge of crisp air. She heard a horse whinny, and she looked in the direction of the corral. Velvet and a couple of other horses were racing about in the enclosure, running first one way, then another, twisting and darting away in still another direction. There was someone standing just inside the half-opened gate; when he glanced towards the house she saw that it was her father. Quickly she slipped off her nightdress and got into her clothes. Fifteen minutes later she tiptoed down the length of the landing to the room at the far end of the floor and poked her head in. John Whitaker arose stiffly, glanced at the blanketed figure on the bed and came out to her. He led her away from the door.

"How is he?" she asked in a low voice.

"Slept the better part o' the night," he told her. "He did some talkin' about that Diane, but all in all I'd say he had a pretty good night."

Her eyes searched his face.

"S'matter?" he asked.

"Have you been to bed at all?"

"Yeah, sure," he said quickly.

"For how long?"

"We-ll, not for too long. Y'see, your father and I kinda spelled each other sittin' up with Kirby. Couple o' hours on, then a couple o' hours off."

"Both of you must be exhausted. You look as though you haven't slept for a week."

He grinned at her.

"G'wan," he said. "Just let me get some breakfast under my belt, and I'll be as good as new."

"What would you like this morning? Bacon and eggs? Ham and eggs?"

"Ham an' eggs."

"I'll let you know when it's ready."

After breakfast Jane suggested that her father and her uncle take a nap. She would see to Kirby's wants, she assured them. They surprised her by accepting her suggestion and acting upon it. They arose heavily and trooped upstairs. She looked in on them shortly after and found them sprawled out on their beds and sleeping soundly. She draped a blanket over each of them, then she went quietly into Kirby's room. He was still fast asleep.

She had cleared the table and had just started to wash

the breakfast dishes when she thought she heard a step outside the house. She went to the back door at once, wiping her hands on a towel she caught up. She opened the door. Hat in hand and looking at her somewhat sheepishly was Lute Bailey.

"Well!" she said. "What do you want here, Lute Bailey? Looking for another unsuspecting victim?"

"Aw, now, Janey, wait a minute," he said protestingly. "I ain't lookin' for anybody. I just want to know about that gun slinger."

"And what do you want to know about him?" she demanded.

"Was he hit bad?"

"Bad enough," she answered coldly. "If you had anything to do with it, I'd advise you to stay far away from him once he's up and about again."

"I didn't do it," he said, and he added earnestly, "Honest, Janey."

She looked at him obliquely.

"Suppose you tell me how you knew he'd been hurt?" she asked.

"I was the one who found him."

Her eyebrows arched.

"Oh," she said. "That's very interesting. Where were you when you found him?"

He averted his eyes.

"Where I shouldn't've been," he answered. "On your side o' the stream."

"Indeed! And what were you doing there?"

His face reddened.

"I was lookin' for you."

"H'm," she said, and his flush deepened.

"He was layin' in the grass just back from the bank," he related. "I was debatin' what to do about him when I saw your father and your uncle comin'. I figgered I'd better get outta there in a hurry, and that's just what I did. I hid away in the brush till they kinda brought him to and got him up on his horse and rode off with him, then I lit out for home."

"You're quite sure you weren't the one who shot him?"

"I didn't do it, I tell you," he said doggedly.

"Then who did?" she demanded.

"I dunno, Janey."

"You'd better get away from here," she said severely, "and you'd better stay away, too."

28

He toyed with his hat, ran his finger around the inside of the sweatband, then his head jerked up.

"I know I shouldn't've come here," he said miserably. "But I just had to."

"Well," she began, and there was a noticeable softening to her tone. But then she checked herself.

"Janey, we aren't as bad as you think we are," he said earnestly. "I know that Pop an' Uncle Giff are kinda hotheaded, and that they don't like bein' pushed around, but——"

"Indeed!" she said icily.

"But they aren't really bad."

"I have things to do," she said loftily. "If that's all you came to say, I'll have to ask you to excuse me."

"I'm sorry I bothered you," he said. "I—I won't do it again."

"Thank you."

"I had kinda hoped you'd understand and that you'd believe me, but if you won't, you won't, and that's all there is to it."

She was motionless, and silent.

" 'Bye," he said.

She did not answer.

He turned slowly and put on his hat, hitched up his belt and tramped away. She closed the door and leaned back against it; after a minute she straightened up and drew a deep breath. Suddenly she sensed the presence of someone else in the room. She turned her head. A gasp broke from her. Standing in the open doorway between the kitchen and the hallway, and leaning against the doorframe for support, was Kirby, a gun gripped in his right hand. He swayed a bit, but he steadied himself almost at once.

"He wasn't the one," he panted.

He seemed to be experiencing some difficulty with his breathing. He sucked in air through his open mouth with a curious, wheezing sound. She came swiftly across the room and looked up at him.

"You shouldn't have done this," she said severely.

"I'm all right," he breathed.

"Please go right back to bed," she insisted.

"I'm all right," he repeated.

He turned slowly. He tottered suddenly, and she sprang to his side and caught him by the arm. He looked down at her for a moment, then he pushed her hand off. He started towards the stairs. He stopped and Jane heard something clatter on the floor. She looked down wonderingly. Then she saw what it was. It was his gun.

Suddenly Kirby sagged brokenly, and although she tried to catch him in her arms, he toppled past her and crashed limply to the floor.

CHAPTER FIVE

GIFF BAILEY came trudging out of the barn and had started up the path towards the house, when he heard the clatter of approaching hoofbeats. He stopped and looked back. The horseman bent low to avoid the sweep of some low-hanging branches that jutted out from the old cotton-wood trees lining the approach to the ranch. When he was past them, he straightened up, and Giff saw that it was Lute. Giff tramped back to the barn door and waited there until his nephew rode up.

"Where've you been?" Giff demanded.

He had such a surly way of talking strangers disliked him without knowing him. Lute swung himself off his horse.

"Out ridin'," he answered.

He led his horse up the short wooden ramp to the barn. Giff backed away a bit to permit them to enter; then he followed them inside. He watched Lute remove his saddle and toss it aside.

"What's the matter with you, boy?" he asked after a minute's silence.

"Nothing," Lute said over his shoulder.

"Somethin's bitin' you," Giff insisted. "An' don't tell me different. You've been moonin' around here lately like a sick calf."

"Pop around?"

"He's in the house. I'm still waitin' for you to tell me what's botherin' you."

The husky youth swung around.

"Awright," he said. "Did you plug that gun slinger the Whitakers've got stayin' at their place?"

Giff frowned.

"Oh," he said. "So that's it!"

"Did you?" Lute repeated.

"Well, supposin' I did plug the no-good so-an'-so? An' mind you, I said supposin'. That any o' your business?"

"I on'y asked you a question," Lute said.

30

"I heard you. But who d'you think you are to ask me questions?"

Lute flushed.

"I've been watchin' you lately, Mister," Giff said thickly. "You're gettin' a mite too big for your britches."

Lute turned on his heel and started out of the barn.

"Wait a minute, damn you!" Giff yelled, and Lute stopped. His uncle came up to him, grabbed him by the arm and spun him around. "When I'm talkin' t' you, you stand still an' listen."

The youth looked at him quietly.

"While I'm tellin' you what's what around here," Giff went on, "here's somethin' else. You stay th' hell away from the Whitakers. Y'hear?"

Lute pushed past him and stalked out of the barn. Giff followed him to the doorway.

"You ain't so big that I can't handle you any more!" he hollered. "You keep on like you've been doin', and I'll paddle the backside offa you. That's a promise!"

Lute tramped up the path to the house. He went in through the back door. His father was pouring a cup of coffee. When the door slammed, he looked up.

"Oh," he said. "Just get back?"

"Couple o' minutes ago," Lute answered.

He took off his hat and scaled it across the room. It soared high, caromed off the far wall and dropped straight down into a chair directly below it. He grunted, sauntered forward to the table and pulled out a chair, swung it around and straddled it. His father seated himself on the other side of the table.

"Pop, did you know that somebody plugged that Whitaker gun slinger?" Lute asked.

Gordon Bailey's eyebrows arched.

"No!" he said. He looked at his son. "You don't think I did it, do you?"

"No," Lute said bluntly. "I don't."

"What was Giff bellowin' about out there?"

"I asked him if he did it, and he flew off the handle," Lute explained. "He wanted to know who I thought I was to ask him questions; then he told me to stay away from the Whitakers. He said a lot o' things, but I walked out on him."

"You didn't answer him back, did you?"

"No, but one o' these days I'll do more'n just answer him back," the youth said darkly.

31

"I wouldn't do that, son," Gordon said. "Giff means well. It's just that he's got a quick temper an' a tongue to match. But you know as well as I do that he'd give you the shirt off his back if you wanted it."

The back door swung open and Giff came in. Gordon looked up at him, but Lute did not move.

"Gordy," Giff said. "You'd better tell this young un o' yours to mind his p's an' q's."

"What'd he do?"

"I don't want 'ny sass outta him. I won't take it."

There was a moment's silence.

"Lute tells me that Whitaker gun slinger's been plugged," Gordon said quietly.

"So what?"

"You know anything about it?"

Giff scowled darkly. "First it was him," he said, jerking his head in Lute's direction. "An' now it's you."

"You did it, didn't you?"

Giff bristled. "Supposin' I did?" he fairly yelled. "What are you gonna do about it?"

"Nothing. I just wanted you to know that I knew who it was that did it."

Giff glared at him. His face was red now, save for two round patches of white that danced into his full cheeks.

"Giff," Gordon said, "I think we've had enough gunplay around here. But we haven't gained anything by it. It hasn't gotten us anywhere either. Let's cut it out."

Giff came up against the table.

"Cut it out—hell! Where d'you think we'd be right this minute if we hadn'ta fought back against the Whitakers, huh? You don't think we'd still be here, do you?"

"I don't know."

"You don't know!" Giff repeated angrily. "Well, I do! We'da lost this place an' every buck we've put into it if you'da had your way! It's a damn good thing I ain't like you. I'll fight f'r what's mine any time. You won't. You c'n get walloped an' still try to make friends with the one who walloped you. Not me!"

"Giff, suppose we go into that another time when you're calmer? Right now there's something else to be discussed, and this is as good a time for it as any."

"Yeah? What is it?"

"I understand you told Lute to stay away from the Whitakers."

"What about it?"

"Just this, Giff. Lute's old enough to be able to choose his own friends."

Giff suddenly smiled. He looked at Lute and smiled at him, then he smiled at Gordon.

" 'Course!" he said, gesturing with both arms. "Why shouldn't he be friends with the Whitakers? For that matter, why shouldn't you be, too? After all, they on'y tried to ruin us. But what's that between friends?" His smile vanished. His face was grim again and hard, almost purplish in colour. "You yellow-bellied swine!" he yelled. "Kowtowin' to the ones who are doin' their damnedest to drive us outta our home! Well, the hell with you an' the hell with them, too! I won't let up on th'm f'r one minute! And if either o' you two get in my way, I'll kick you both off the place!"

His eyes were bulging; he was panting, too. He looked from one to the other.

"From now on," he yelled, and he pounded the table with his fist, "from now on, I'm runnin' things around here. You two'll do as I say, or off you go. G'wan! Get outta here! Get outta my sight!"

Neither Gordon nor Lute moved.

"Get outta here, y' hear?" Giff screamed. "Or are you both deaf?"

He whirled suddenly and struck at Lute, who pulled back and went sprawling on the floor. Giff kicked him and Lute twisted away. Gordon was on his feet now. He came around the table and tried to pull his brother away, but Giff, wheeling, lashed out at him, struck him several times in the face and sent him reeling. Lute scrambled to his feet. He came plunging foward. Giff, cursing, turned to meet him. Lute struck him savagely, with the full power of his strong young body behind each punch. He drove his uncle across the room. Giff collided heavily with a chair, fell over it, grabbed at it frantically in an effort to save himself from falling. The chair went down with him. Gordon Bailey leaped forward. He tried to stop his son, but Lute pushed him off, pulled the chair away from Giff's tangled legs and stood over him with his big fists clenched.

"Get up!" he yelled. "Get up an' I'll kill you!"

Gordon threw his arms around his son and managed to drag him away.

Slowly, Giff climbed to his feet. His left eye was swollen. There was a deepening angry red welt on his jaw and his mouth was puffy. He spat out something; it rolled across the floor. He glowered at Lute.

"I'm gonna fix you for this," he said thickly.

"You just try it," the youth said grimly.

"Lute!" Gordon said. "That's enough!"

"Awright, Pop."

"You'd better go outside, Son."

Lute nodded, turned and sauntered out of the house.

"This place ain't big enough f'r all uv us now," Giff said.

"You brought it on yourself, Giff."

"You buy me out," Giff said, "or I'll buy out."

"I haven't got the money to do that," Gordon said. "You know that."

"Then I'll buy you out. Get your stuff t'gether, an' we'll ride right into town an' get it settled. But I want it done t'day! I don't want either o' you around here any longer'n you have to be!"

"All right," Gordon said quietly. He went swiftly to the door. "Lute!"

Lute filled the doorway.

"Yeah, Pop?"

"We're selling our interest in the ranch, Son," Gordon said. "Come upstairs and help me pack our things."

Lute's eyes were wide with surprise.

"Y'mean we're sellin' out to him?" he asked, nodding in Giff's direction.

Gordon nodded.

"Well, what d'you know!" Lute said as he came into the house again. Giff glared at him. "Ol' buzzard," Lute said, as he passed him on the way to the stairs.

Jake Holloway was coming out of the bank when the three Baileys pulled up in front of it. He nodded to them and started away; he stopped suddenly and retraced his steps. He looked up at Giff for a moment and whistled.

"Holy cow, Giff!" he exclaimed. "What in thunder happened t' you?"

Lute grinned and looked away.

Giff dismounted stiffly, shouldered Jake out of his way and stalked into the bank.

"What'd he do?" Jake asked Gordon as the latter climbed down from his horse. "Tangle with a mountain lion, or was it a buzz saw? Or did he let his horse walk on 'im?"

"Jake," Lute said, "d'you know where I can get a job?"

Jake looked up at him. There was surprise in his eyes.

"Huh?" he said. "Ain't you with your father an' your Uncle Giff any more?"

Lute shook his head.

"Pop's selling out to Uncle Giff," he answered.

"Oh!" Jake said. "So that's how it is!"

"Yep," Lute said. "That's how it is."

"Jake," Gordon said, "you get around. You hear things. We're lookin' for a small spread. Just for Lute an' me. Know of one we can pick up cheap?"

"Heard somebody say that Pete Willis wants to sell his place," the stocky stagecoach operator answered. "Why don't you an' Lute ride out an' see him?"

"Where's his place?" Gordon asked.

"I dunno. But I oughta be able to find out. Look, if I ain't around when you get finished in here, chances are you c'n find me over to th' Western."

"We'll look for you," Gordon said.

"You do that."

"Come on, Son," Gordon said, "let's go inside."

Half an hour later, when they came out of the bank, they found Jake waiting for them on the pavement. He led them over to the kerb.

"You don't want any part o' Willis' spread," he informed them.

"How come?" Lute asked.

"I asked a couple o' fellers who know Willis," Jake explained. "They all told me th' same thing. Land's hilly an' stony and water just ain't."

"Oh," Gordon said, plainly disappointed.

"Which is prob'ly why Mister Willis wants to unload what he's got," Jake concluded. He brightened suddenly. "Look. I've got another idea. Y'know, we never elected another sheriff to take Lew Finney's place when he got sick an' died. Well, just the other night some o' the businessmen in town got together. Seems they don't like bein' without some kind o' protection in view o' the newcomers who've been driftin' into town these last couple o' weeks. We're gonna get us a sheriff."

"That's not for me," Gordon said.

"How d'you know it ain't?" Jake retorted.

Gordon shook his head.

"Look," Jake said. "Why don't you let me tell you about the job before you say 'no'—huh? You c'n always turn it down afterward, y'know. It might be, after you've heard

35

me out an' you've had a chance to sleep on it, you'll feel different about it an' wanna give it a try."

"Sure," Lute said quickly.

"Well," Gordon said, "all right."

"It's this way," Jake began. "We c'n afford t' do awright for a sheriff. Now if you was to take the job, you could still keep lookin' around for a place. When you find it, you'll have more money than you've got now, so you'll be able t' put more into it. Get it? Soon's you're set, you turn in your badge an' go back to ranchin'. What's the matter with that?"

"Wait a minute," Lute said. "What's the matter with me? Ain't the sheriff supposed t' have a deputy?"

Jake grinned at him. "It could be," he said.

"Well?" Lute demanded.

"Suppose you gimme a chance to talk to th' others?" Jake suggested.

"How soon d'we hafta say 'yes' or 'no'?" Lute wanted to know.

"Soon's I ask you. That'll be maybe two or three days. It'll take me a little time to get some o' the others to agree to raisin' th' figger we decided on for the sheriff. Some o' th'm'd sooner give their blood than their dough."

"Think you c'n swing it?" Lute asked.

"I think so," Jake answered. "I c'n out-holler every last one o' th'm, and usually, in an argument, y'know—and this'll be one sure as shootin'—the feller who c'n keep talkin' the loudest an' the longest wins."

Giff Bailey emerged from the bank at that moment. He strode straight to the kerb, pushed Jake out of his way, untied his horse and climbed up on him, wheeled and rode off.

"H'm," Jake said. "See you fellers later."

"We'll be around," Lute said. They saw Jake go into the Western, then Lute turned to his father. "Hey, Pop, y'know somethin'?"

"What?"

"I'm hungry. What d'you say we go get ourselves somethin' to eat?"

CHAPTER SIX

THE buckboard came whirling around the house and braked to a noisy stop at the back door.

"Jim!" John Whitaker called as he climbed down from the driver's seat. "Hey, Jim!"

The door opened, and John looked up.

"Uncle John—please!" Jane said from the doorway.

"S'matter? Oh . . . Kirby asleep?"

"He was."

Jim Whitaker came striding around the house.

"Get everything?" he asked.

"Yep," his brother answered. "Everything you had on that list an' then some."

"What d'you mean, 'an' then some'?"

"I mean that I got th' groceries and an earful o' news."

"I'm listenin'."

"All right. Don't go 'way, Jane. I know you'll be interested in this, too. First off, we've finally got us a new sheriff."

"Y'don't say!" Jim said. "Who is he, John? A stranger or somebody we all know?"

John frowned. "His name's Bailey. Gordon Bailey."

"Oh, no!" Jane said in shocked tones.

"Oh, yes!" John said grimly. "And who d'you suppose he's got f'r deputy? Lute."

"How'd that all come about?" Jim asked. "What about the Bailey ranch?"

"Gordon sold out to Giff."

"Too bad it wasn't the other way around," Jim said. "Gordy ain't so bad. It's Giff who's the ornery one."

"I'll bet he's a heap worse now than he ever was."

"Why?"

"Well, accordin' to the way I got it, it seems there was some kind o' fight out at the Bailey place. The three o' them rode into the town, an' Jake Holloway saw them. He said Giff's face looked like it'd been chewed up."

"That's funny," Jim said. "Who d'you suppose did it to him? Gordy?"

"Nobody seems t' know."

"That Lute's a husky young feller," Jim mused. "Wonder if he did it?"

"What difference does it make who gave Giff a good wallopin'? Long's he was the one who got walloped, I'm satisfied. Oh, yeah. Here's somethin' else. Giff's hired a feller named Al Branch."

"Branch?" Jim repeated.

"Yeah."

"Branch," Jim said again thoughtfully. "I've heard that name before."

"Jake told me the same thing."

"Wait a minute," Jim said. "I've got it. Must be ten, twelve years ago. This Al Branch killed a lawman, a ranger, I think it was. Anyway, he went off to prison."

"That's nice."

Jim looked troubled.

"What's the matter?" John asked.

"I wish it was Giff who'd sold out 'stead of Gordy. Long as Giff's around we'll always have trouble. And if he hires any more men like that Branch, we're gonna be in for it."

It was probably a week later that John Whitaker made another trip to town and, when he returned, he was grim-faced. However, this time he halted the buckboard in front of the barn and sought out his brother.

"How come you didn't take that stuff up to the house?" Jim asked.

"Wanted to see you alone. Didn't want Janey to hear this."

Jim looked at him. "What is it?" he asked.

"Giff's hired a playmate for that Al Branch. Feller named Coady. Understand he comes fr'm Texas. He's supposed to be somethin' of a bad man."

"Uh-huh. Go on, John."

"Some o' the folks in town don't like the idea o' Giff's hirin' out-an-out troublemakers, an' they've had a meeting about it. They put it up to Gordy, but they know he won't do anything much about it. He ain't the man for the job. They should've hired a stranger, a younger man, one who could handle somethin' like this."

Jim made no comment.

"Couple o' men, Jake Holloway, Ed Truscott, Tom Hanley an' some others went to see Beardsley down at the bank, figgerin' that if Giff owed the bank any money an' didn't pay up when it was due, Beardsley could get tough with him an' tell him the only way the bank would give him 'n extension o' time would be if he got rid o' Branch an' Coady."

"What happened? How'd they make out?"

John shook his head. "Giff owes the bank some money, but he pays his interest right smack on th' due date. So Beardsley can't do anything to help."

"There oughta be some way o' handlin' Giff."

"If you've got an idea, Holloway and the others'll be doggoned glad to hear about it."

"I was only talkin'."

"That's all right. But maybe you can figger out somethin'. It'll be a heap easier on us if you can, Jim, than if we have to handle Giff an' his hired hands by ourselves. If we were younger, I'd look forward to tanglin' with Giff. I'm sixty-two, an' while I hate like th' dickens to admit it, I ain't the man I was twenty-five years ago."

Jim smiled. "If it's any consolation to you, John—who is?"

John didn't answer. He shook his head, then he climbed up into the buckboard, unwound the reins from around the brake handle and drove around the house to the back door.

Days went by, a week; then another week came and went. Kirby was permitted to get about. The Whitakers' only easy chair was carried out of the parlour and set up on an open, grassy stretch of ground. Instructed to "sit out there and soak in some of that good, warm sunshine," Kirby obeyed. The sun made him feel good; it also made him drowsy. He was dozing, slumped back in the chair, his long legs stretched out in front of him, when Jane came out of the house and across the grass to where he was sitting.

"Mr. Kirby," she said.

His eyes opened.

"Oh," he said. He drew in his legs, shifted himself into a more normal sitting position.

"Your milk," she said. "Here."

He looked at the tall glass in her hand, then he shook his head.

"What's the matter?" Jane asked.

"You've spoiled me so beautifully these last two weeks, how will I get along when I'm alone again and dependent upon myself?"

She smiled fleetingly.

"Oh, you'll manage. I'm sure you will."

"Perhaps. But it won't be the same. I can tell that already."

She held out the glass to him. He took it and balanced it on his knee.

"Would you like something with the milk, Mr. Kirby?"

He shook his head. "No, thank you," he said. "Would you mind very much if I asked you to call me Vance?"

"Not at all."

"Thank you. May I call you Jane?"

"If you like."

He looked at her for a moment.

"Are you very busy?" he asked. "I mean, is there something you must attend to right away?"

"No. Nothing that can't wait. Why?"

"Would you talk to me?"

"What about?"

"You."

"I'm not a very interesting topic."

"You're being unnecessarily modest."

"Very well," she said. "Just what do you want to know about me?"

He looked down at the grass; she followed his eyes, then she sat down at his feet.

"You aren't at all like any of the girls or women I've known or met," he began. "You're far prettier than any of them, yet you're so much more down to earth. Tell me about yourself."

"It will be very brief because my life hasn't been a very exciting one," she said. "I've lived on a ranch ever since I can remember. My mother died when I was born, and my father raised me. My uncle came to live with us when I was very young—when I was about three, I think, or perhaps four. He's been with us ever since. I've never really known any women. I've lived all my life among men. I—I think that's about all there is to tell you."

"There must be a lot of things you'd like to know about me."

"Oh, I don't know! What makes you think that?"

"Well, for one thing, you've never known anyone quite like me, have you?"

She shook her head.

"Then doesn't that make you all the more curious to know why I'm so different?"

She did not answer. She toyed with a blade of grass, curled it around her finger.

"I think you were horrified when I first came here. The thought of having a hired killer in your midst sickened and disgusted you, didn't it? But then, after a while, you began to notice that I wasn't very much different from other people, at least outwardly. It probably bothered you because you had actually seen me kill a man. You didn't know that I saw you up at that window, did you? I did though. You tried to do things for me in a totally indifferent way, but you found you couldn't. And because you couldn't, your curiosity increased. You didn't want to know anything about me, yet you had to. I could tell it. It was in your eyes. How many times I found you staring at me, wondering about me, wondering what went on inside of me that made me a man apart from other men!"

Her eyes lifted and focused on a white, billowing cloud; she watched it for a minute, intently, afraid to look at him.

"I was in the army before I came out here," he went on. "I was stationed in Arizona. I liked army life. I'd intended making it my life's work. When I resigned my commission it was the end of me."

"Why—why did you leave the service?"

He did not answer right away.

She looked directly at him. "Why did you resign?" she asked.

His face grew grim, almost forbidding.

"I got into a mess over a woman," he said bitterly.

"Oh!"

"It wasn't what you're thinking. I wasn't in love with her."

"Was her name Diane?"

"Yes," he said. There was surprise in his voice. "How did you know?"

"You talked about a Diane several times when you were delirious."

"Oh," he said. "She was the wife of another officer, my best friend. She wasn't in love with him, although he was with her. She wanted to get away from him, and—well—I happened to be handy, and incidentally, unmarried. She practically threw herself at me. Understand me, please—she wasn't unattractive—but there are things a man will do and things he won't do. Anyway, she and Rod quarrelled one day, bitterly, and she taunted him, told

41

him I'd asked her to go away with me. When she flounced out of their quarters, he killed himself."

Jane averted her eyes quickly; she felt she could make the telling easier for him if she did not look at him.

"I resigned my commission and came out here. She followed me, pleaded with me to marry her. She had no money, nothing. Her family and her friends had disowned her." He stopped and drew a deep breath. "I married her. But she tired of me quickly and left me for another man, a fellow named Trevvett. When he walked out on her, she came back to me, begging to be forgiven. We quarrelled, and I lost my head and struck her. I went out and got drunk. I ran into Trevvett and got into a fight with him and, when he pulled a knife on me, I killed him. I got away all right, but I had to shoot my way to freedom. In the course of my getaway, I killed one of my pursuers. From then on I didn't care about anything, where I went or what I did. I couldn't work because I couldn't do justice to myself or the job. I kept moving about, but there isn't any escape from one's memories. It was only when I got good and drunk that I had any peace. Then she and Rod and Trevvett and that other fellow didn't appear to plague me."

Vance sank back in the chair. Jane got up on her knees and looked at him closely. She took the glass of milk out of his hand and set it down in the grass.

"Don't talk any more," she said. "It doesn't do you any good."

"I wanted you to know," he answered. "Let me finish. There isn't very much more. When I met your uncle, I was broke. We got to talking and, when he told me about the man the Baileys were bringing to town, I offered to take the job of protecting your father. I had nothing to lose. If I were killed—what of it? If I killed the other fellow and thus saved your father's life, then the money paid me was well spent. When the job was done, I'd go on my way. I didn't plan to stay on here any longer than the job required. I didn't plan to get shot up like this either."

There was a clatter of hoofs, and Jane got up on her feet. Jim Whitaker rode up.

He looked at Jane, then at Kirby.

"Jane," he called. "Come inside a minute."

He dismounted and went into the house. A minute later Jane came in.

"Yes, Dad?"

"Jane," her father began. "You aren't fallin' in love with Kirby, are you?"

"Why, Dad!"

"I just don't want you to get hurt," Jim said.

"Silly!" Jane said with a light laugh.

"Maybe. It's just that I've seen the doggonedest things happen. The reason I mentioned it is that I don't want to see any o' them happen to you. That's all. You'd better go back to Kirby now. It won't look right 'less you do."

CHAPTER SEVEN

THE half curtain that hung so lifelessly over the lower part of Giff Bailey's kitchen window was faded and worn; the pane of glass it covered was smudged and dust-streaked. Giff used the curtain to wipe the pane so that he might see through it. He let the curtain fall back in place, then he lifted a corner of it and peered out. While he wanted to see the two men who were leaning over the corral gate, he did not want them to know that he was watching them. Their backs were turned to him; though he could not see their faces, he took it for granted that they were talking. He wondered what they were talking about; not knowing disturbed him. He did not feel comfortable with both of them around. It made him wonder if he had done the right thing in hiring the second man.

Branch, the heavier one of the two, did not worry him. True, the man had a bad reputation; still he went about his work with an eagerness to please that made Giff nod approvingly. The fellow was probably grateful for the opportunity given him to work and earn a living. He had doubtless experienced a lot of difficulty in getting anyone to consider him for a job; Giff's willingness to take a chance on him had heartened him, and his eagerness was proof of it.

It was upon the second man, Dave Coady, that Giff's eyes focused. The man was tall and lean and dark and thin-faced, with quick, flashing eyes. It was his eyes that bothered Giff most; they seemed to blaze much too suddenly, an indication of a quick temper and a reckless nature. The fact that he, himself, was hot-tempered had nothing to do with his appraisal of another. Giff was the boss. He could be anything he liked, and no one could criticize him.

But a quick-tempered employee—that was different. Coady, he decided, would be the one to get him into trouble. He would watch the man, and fire him the moment he showed signs of getting out of hand. That would be the end of it.

Of course, Giff admitted, it could be that they weren't talking about him at all. There was that possibility. But since there was a doubt in his mind, it made him uneasy. Suppose they were talking about him? What could they be saying? Could it be a plot to take his ranch away from him? He thought about it for a moment, then he shook his head. No, he was safe on that point. The ranch was registered in his name, and so was the title to it. Could it be a discussion of his money? He thought about that, too. He didn't keep enough cash on hand to make stealing it worth anyone's while. It was a pretty-well-accepted fact that ranchers seldom had much cash on hand, and he was satisfied that both Branch and Coady had been around long enough to know that he was no exception to the rule. He felt relieved, now that he had considered the two most important topics they might be discussing. He dropped the curtain and turned away from the window.

Could it be that they were talking about the Whitakers? He had told both Branch and Coady about his difficulties with his neighbours. He had denounced them bitterly. Coady, he recalled, had smiled. If the Whitakers were that ornery, he had asked, why hadn't Giff really done something about them? After all, there were ways and ways of squaring accounts with troublesome and unreasonable neighbours. That reminded him, Coady had continued, of an outfit in the Texas panhandle. They had caused a lot of trouble among their neighbours; then one day some of them got together, made their plans and swooped down upon the offenders. There was a brief fight. The defenders were bullet-riddled, and the torch was put to their place. Of course, Coady had added quickly, it didn't follow that the Whitakers needed such drastic treatment; if they were just troublesome, perhaps something in the way of punishment could be cooked up. Just how far could they go against the Whitakers? he had asked. Giff recalled that he had roared his answer—they could go as far as they pleased. Coady's eyebrows had arched. Then, smiling, he had patted the butt of his gun and sauntered out.

Now Giff wondered if he shouldn't have modified his

reply. It was one thing for him to feel bitter about his neighbours; it was another to let a couple of strangers, trigger-happy strangers at that, take things into their own hands. He would be the one responsible for their actions. Giff frowned as he trudged upstairs.

"Did you get t' know a feller named Haskell where you were?" Coady asked.

"Haskell?" Branch repeated. "Nope."

"Understood he was doin' time there, too," Coady went on. "He was a swell feller awright. You'da liked him."

"I didn't get to know many o' the men there," Branch explained. "Soon's they saw you gettin' a little friendly with any o' them, they moved you."

"Uh-huh," Coady said. "How d'you like workin' for Bailey?"

"Oh, awright," Branch replied. "He ain't a bad sort. He's a little hotheaded, an' he likes to holler some, but outside o' that he's awright."

"I'm kinda surprised he never went after them Whitakers an' really gave it to th'm."

Branch shrugged. "Maybe he'll hafta one o' these days," he said. "If they act up again, chances are Bailey won't let it pass this time."

Coady smiled. "If Haskell was here," he said, "there wouldn't be any waitin'. When he didn't like anybody, he just went after th'm."

Branch was silent.

"I took a ride along the fence yesterday," Coady went on. "Them Whitakers got some nice-lookin' steers, but fr'm what Bailey tells me, they don't have anybody t' ride their fence. Both o' the Whitakers are white-haired, gettin' on in years."

"I know."

"I swung south," Coady continued. "There's a pass that leads through the hills."

Branch turned his head and looked at him.

"What are you gettin' at?" he asked.

"Nuthin," Coady said calmly. "You got 'ny dough?"

"I've been in prison for ten years," Branch answered.

"Have 'ny trouble findin' a job?"

"And how," Branch said grimly. "Soon's they found out I'd been in prison, nobody wanted any part o' me. That is, everybody but Bailey."

"Uh-huh. Ever think o' goin' to California? New country, new people. A feller's really got a chance to make somethin' uv 'imself out there."

"For ten years I thought o' nothing else but California. But I haven't 'ny dough, an' without dough what chance has anyone o' gettin' there?"

"Yeah, that'd be the place for you, Branch."

"I'd give anything to get out there."

Coady looked at him. "I wonder," he said.

"What d'you mean?"

"Just what I said," Coady retorted. "In this life the man who won't help himself is plumb outta luck. Nobody else is gonna do anything for him if he won't do it for himself."

"You're hintin' at somethin', Coady. Why don't you come out with it?"

"Awright. I got some friends south o' here. They're pretty well connected. If I get my hands on somethin' worth-while, they're always ready to take it over for me, an' pay me well for my trouble."

"Uh-huh," Branch said. "That include cattle?"

"It includes anything that they c'n make a profit on."

"I see."

"You interested?"

"I dunno. I gotta think about it."

"Awright. On'y one thing, Branch."

"What's that?"

"Think about it all you like," Coady said with a smile. "But don't talk about it. Get the idea?"

"Yeah, sure."

"Swell. See you later."

They separated. Branch tramped off towards the barn while Coady went into the bunkhouse.

It was probably an hour later, as Coady was riding slowly along the fence that separated the Bailey and Whitaker ranches, that he heard approaching hoofbeats. He pulled his horse to a stop and twisted around in his saddle. Al Branch gestured to him, and Coady wheeled away from the fence and rode forward to meet him.

"Been lookin' all over for you," Branch said, easing himself in his saddle.

Coady smiled again. "Looks like you knew where to find me," he answered.

"What's the deal?"

Coady turned and pointed to a bunch of cattle grazing a short distance beyond the fence.

"There it is," he said, turning again. "About a hundred an' eighty head o' the best-lookin' cattle anyone ever saw."

Branch stood up in his stirrups for a moment, then he nodded and sat down again.

"What d'you figger they're worth?" he asked.

"Y'mean to us?"

" 'Course."

"Oh, five thousand. Maybe more."

"That'd make it twenty-five hundred apiece."

"That's right," Coady said. "Are you plannin' to take a hand in the deal?"

"Looks like it, don't it?"

Coady laughed.

"Looks like it, sure," he answered. "But looks don't always mean 'yes'. Sometimes they on'y mean 'maybe'."

"I'm goin' in on it," Branch said.

"That's what I've been waitin' to hear you say."

"What do we do?"

"Right now we don't do anything. Soon's I get word from those parties I told you about, we'll get movin'. I'll let you know soon's I know."

"Awright," Branch said. He wheeled his horse. "I'd better be hustlin' back. Don't want the boss to get suspicious."

"Right. I'll hang back for a while; then when I figger you're there, I'll head back, too."

The next two days were uneventful ones. It was late in the afternoon of the third day when Coady came sauntering into the barn. Branch was on his knees, plying a hammer on some floor-board nails that had come loose. He looked up when he heard Coady's step. Coady watched him for a moment.

"You're a good man with a hammer," he said aloud. "Those nails are gonna stay put when you get finished with th'm. If I was doin' that job, chances are f'r every wallop I landed on a nail head, I'd land one on one o' my fingers."

He looked around.

"Where's the boss?" he asked in a somewhat lower tone of voice.

"In the house."

Coady dropped to one knee beside Branch.

"We're goin' ridin' tonight," he said. "We'll say somethin' about goin' to town, then right after supper we'll get goin'. When we're far enough away from here, we'll circle back to the fence, cut through and get those steers and drive th'm south to the pass."

Branch nodded, raised the hammer and drove a last nail into the flooring.

"From there on," Coady continued, "they take over."

"When do we get the dough?"

"Tonight."

Branch climbed to his feet. Coady came erect, too.

"See you later," he said. He patted Branch on the back and strolled out.

Supper was nearly over when Coady turned to Branch.

"How about ridin' into town with me tonight?" he asked.

"Oh, I dunno. Anything special doin' there?"

Coady smiled. "You might be surprised," he said. He looked at Giff and winked. "Tell him about those dance-hall girls, Boss."

Giff frowned.

"There's one girl," Coady went on. "A redhead. An' is she somethin'! Man, wait'll you get a look at her, Branch. You'll fall for her same's everybody else. I understand she's got a list a foot long o' men who wanna marry her. We might as well add our names to it. Huh?"

"Not interested," Branch said. "But I'll ride in with you because I c'n use a couple o' shirts. The ones I've got are fallin' apart. When d'you wanna go?"

"Soon's you're ready," Coady replied. "Awright with you, Boss, if we get goin'?"

Giff grunted. Coady and Branch got up from the table, picked up their hats and went out. Giff watched them from the window, saw them go into the barn. A minute later they came out astride their horses. Giff retraced his steps to the table.

"That Coady," he muttered. "I don't like that maverick. One o' these days I'm gonna light on him, an' that'll be the end o' him far as this outfit's concerned. He's just a little too cute for me."

CHAPTER EIGHT

THE Oasis Café was alive with voices, laughter and the tinkling of piano keys. The bar was crowded; the tables beyond it, along the side and rear walls were crowded, too. A package under his arm, Al Branch eased himself into a spot at the bar; he turned his head and let his eyes range the length of the place. There was no sign of Coady. Then he happened to look upward. There was a narrow balcony above the main floor, and coming out of a room that opened up on it was a laughing redheaded girl. A step behind her was Coady.

"What'll it be, Mister?" the bartender asked.

Branch jerked his head around.

"Rye," he answered, and he turned again. Coady and the girl came down the single flight of stairs. Coady pinched the girl's cheek, turned away and came forward to the bar.

"Hi," he said, stopping at Branch's side. "How you doin'?"

"Oh, awright," Branch answered. "Looks like you were doin' awright for yourself, too."

Coady smiled. "Get a look at 'er?" he asked. The bartender placed a drink in front of Branch. "Hey, what about me?"

"Rye?"

"Yeah, a double shot," Coady said. The bartender moved away. Coady nudged Branch. "How'd you like 'er?"

"You know how to pick th'm."

Coady laughed. "Don't I though? But pickin' th'm ain't all. You've gotta have that certain somethin' that women go for, an' from the results I get, it looks like I've got it," he said. The bartender returned, placed a drink on the bar in front of Coady. The latter dug in his pocket, drew out a silver dollar and dropped it on the bar. "Take it outta that, Mac, an' keep the change."

"Thanks, Mister."

Coady picked up his glass.

"Here's mud in your eye," he said. He touched his glass to Branch's. They downed their drinks and put down the empty glasses. "Let's go."

They went out to the street, untied their horses, climbed up on them and rode down the street. Coady twisted around and looked back. He laughed and waved his hand. Branch looked back, too. The redheaded girl was waving from the doorway of the Oasis. They settled down in their saddles, quickened their pace as they left the town behind them.

"How d'you feel now?" Coady asked, turning to Branch.

"Awright, I guess," Branch answered. "A little jumpy but nuthin' to worry about."

"Oughta feel good to know you've got some real dough in your pocket for a change," Coady remarked.

"It does, believe me."

"When was the last time you had twenty-five hundred bucks all at one time?"

"There never was a time like that," Branch said. "Look, how soon d'you think we'll be able to pull outta here?"

"Oh, in a week or so."

"Hope I last that long. Waitin' around always gets me."

"Come on, Branch! You haven't got a blamed thing t' worry about," Coady urged. "Nobody can connect us with the Whitaker cattle. We haven't got th'm. Somebody just took th'm, an' that's that. Let them look anywhere they like. They won't find 'ny trace o' th'm. By tomorrow mornin' Gillen's boys will have fixed th' brands on those steers so that nobody—not even the Whitakers—will be able t' tell th'm from Gillen's regular stock. On top o' that, he's shippin' out eleven hundred head in a couple o' days, an' the Whitaker steers'll be among th'm."

"Sounds awright," Branch admitted.

"It is awright," Coady insisted. "Gillen's a smart operator. He can't afford to get into anything that don't look right, so you know doggoned well he's gonna do his part to make everything look just so. Quit worryin', will you? If you hafta worry, wait till you've got somethin' that needs worryin' about."

"When we do get ready to hightail it," Branch said, "what'll we tell Bailey?"

"Just that I got us a couple o' swell jobs in Texas, an' that we're takin' th'm. Anything wrong with that? C'n anybody hate us for takin' better jobs that pay us a helluva lot o' more dough?"

"When'll you tell him that we're quittin'?"

"In a couple o' days. I'm expectin' a letter, an' when I get it I'll let him see it."

"I don't get it. Y'mean somebody's sendin' you a letter offerin' us jobs?"

Coady laughed. "That's right," he said. "The on'y trouble with it is that one o' my friends is writin' the letter and mailin' it from Texas to make it look good. Get the idea now?"

"Sure. Y'know somethin', Coady?"

"What?"

"How come you're wastin' all th' talent you've got on small stuff like this?"

"I won't always waste it!"

"No, I suppose not."

"Come on," Coady said. "Let's step on it. We don't wanna keep Bailey up all night wonderin' where we are."

They lashed their horses and sent them bounding ahead.

When they reached the ranch and pulled up in front of the barn, the back door of the house slammed, and Giff, a lighted lantern swinging from his hand, came down the path.

"H'llo, Boss," Coady said, dismounting.

"Finally got back, eh?"

"Yep. Had us a little time in town, an' when we had enough, we hightailed it."

Giff looked at Branch.

"What's that package you've got there?" he demanded.

"Just a couple o' work shirts I bought," Branch replied.

"Yeah? How do I know there ain't a couple o' bottles o' whisky in there instead?"

Coady laughed. Giff whirled and glared at him. Coady suddenly found something of interest in the sky.

"Wanna see the shirts?" Branch asked.

"You'd better show th'm to him," Coady said. "On'y I hope for your sake, Branch, that they ain't the kind he likes or you're gonna be plumb outta luck."

Giff set the lantern on the ground between his feet. Branch handed him the package. Giff ripped it open, fumbled with the paper and clutched at two denim shirts that fell out, eluded his hand and dropped at his feet. He cursed, threw the paper at Branch, caught up the lantern, wheeled and stalked up the path. Coady laughed softly and led his horse into the barn. Branch came in behind him with the shirts folded up under his arm. When they had unsaddled their horses, they sauntered out of the barn and tramped off towards the bunkhouse.

"If he ain't the damnedest feller," Coady said. Branch went in ahead of him and struck a match. Presently a light flamed in the lamp that stood on the makeshift table. Coady closed the door behind him, leaned back against it. "Y'know, he could get under my skin awful fast. I hope t' hell he don't act up while we're still here. I wouldn't wanna hafta push his face in."

"Better lock the door," Branch suggested.

"Huh? Oh, yeah," Coady said. He turned, pushed the bolt home, then he unbuckled his gun belt and slung it on his bunk. "I'm tired. I could sleep for a week. How 'bout you?"

"Oh, I'll sleep awright. My legs an' my backside are sore. I did more ridin' tonight than I've done in a heck uva long time."

Coady undressed first, pushed his gun belt under his pillow, got into his bunk and pulled up the covers.

"Open that window a little, will you?" he asked.

"Sure."

Coady turned over on his side, his face to the wall. A minute later his heavy breathing indicated that he was asleep. Branch bent over him, looked at him, shook his head as he straightened up again.

"What a man!" he muttered.

He turned out the light. Then, remembering that he hadn't opened the window, groped his way to it, pushed it open. Retracing his steps to his bunk, he stumbled over his own boots and cursed when he stubbed his toe. But presently he was in his bunk. A heavy silence settled over the bunkhouse; it reached out shortly and draped itself over the barn and the house, stilling every sound within its folds.

Jane did not sleep very well that night. She tossed and turned and burrowed deep into her bed; still sleep did not come to her. Finally, she kicked off the covers, pushed her feet into her bed slippers, and groped her way to the window and opened it wide. The night air was crisp and bracing. She breathed it in deeply. She knelt down, resting her arms on the low window sill, her back and her head against the window frame. She looked skyward. There was a bright moon overhead and a sky full of stars. She moved her head a bit. The bunkhouse and tool shed was dark and shadowy. The barn was dark, too, but in the distorting night light it loomed up even bigger than it was. She looked in the direction of the corral. The worn bars gleamed with an unnatural whiteness. Then she sank back again. Vance Kirby's face came into her thoughts. She smiled when she recalled her father's words. She wasn't in love with Vance Kirby. She was certain of it, so certain that the very idea amused her. There was, she admitted, a certain fascination about the man: he was good-looking, he was obviously an educated man—but that

52

was all. Certainly his calling was about as unattractive as anything could be. Then there was the matter of a wife somewhere in the offing. In love with him, with a man who had killed three other men and who would probably kill many more before he was finished? She got up, drew down the window and went back to bed.

She felt chilled now, and she drew the covers high around her. She turned on her side and buried her face in the pillow. After a while she dozed off, but her sleep was short lived; she turned on her back, then she twisted over on her side again. She slept in fits and starts, awoke each time more annoyed than the time before. Finally, she sat up and made a light in the lamp and picked up a book. She read for a while, put down the book and closed her eyes; she opened them again and turned out the light and slid down beneath the covers.

She awoke with a start when she heard voices. She sat up, blinked in the bright sun that was streaming into her room. She got out of bed and went swiftly across the room to the window. She could see a tall, lean man—Kirby —leaning over the corral gate. She wondered where her father and her uncle were; it was their voices that she heard. Then they appeared. Her father was leading his horse. The animal, she noticed, was glistening with perspiration, an indication that he had been doing some fast running. Kirby turned as they came up to him. There was some talk; her father seemed unusually agitated about something, and she wondered what it was. Then he turned suddenly and climbed up on his horse.

"We'll see, by God!" she heard him say.

He wheeled, lashed his horse and sent him thundering away. Kirby and her uncle talked for another minute, then they turned away from the corral and started towards the house. They stopped once and talked in low tones, then they went on again. Jane draped the curtain around her and poked her head out of the window.

"Uncle John!" she called.

He looked up.

"What is it?" she asked. "What's happened?"

He shook his head. "Nothing for you to worry your head about," he answered.

"Where did Dad go?"

"To town," Uncle John answered.

She withdrew her head, dropped the curtain and quickly skimmed out of her nightdress and into her clothes.

When she came downstairs, some ten minutes later, Kirby and her uncle were standing just outside the back door. She dropped a pan, and Uncle John opened the door and looked in.

"Y'mean we're gonna have some breakfast after all?" he asked.

Jane bowed her head. "I'm ashamed of myself," she said. "Thoroughly ashamed, too. All I can say is that I overslept and that I'm sorry. Incidentally, before I'm punished for my crime, what time is it?"

"Half past nine."

"Goodness!" Jane said.

"You holler when you want us to come in."

"I will . . . Oh, Uncle John!"

"Yeah?"

"Why did Dad go off to town so hurriedly?"

"He went to see the new sheriff."

"The new sheriff?" she repeated. Then her lip curled. "Oh, Gordon Bailey!"

"You mean you remember him?"

"Much too well," she retorted. "But why did Dad want to see him?"

"Seems we've got us some trouble."

"With Giff Bailey?"

"I dunno f'r sure, Janey. But chances are he or his hired hands had somethin' to do with it."

"With what?" she demanded impatiently. "What is this trouble you're talking about?"

"Somebody cut our fence an' ran off some of our stock."

"Oh!" she said, and her face clouded.

"But like I said before, young un," he said, "don't you go worryin' y'self over it. We'll get to the bottom of it. You can bet on it."

The door closed again. For a minute she was motionless. So Giff had struck at them. Now she understood why he had hired a man like that Branch. It was all so clear to her. Giff had had Kirby shot down in order to clear the way for what he probably felt would be an all-out attack on the Whitakers, one that would finish them off once and for all. Then a cold smile toyed at the corners of her mouth. Giff hadn't reckoned too well. Kirby was well again. Evidently Giff didn't know that; the fact that he had struck at them so boldly was proof of it. She gloated over it. The smile deepened. Kirby would be equal to the situation. He would take good care of Mister Branch.

54

Perhaps, if he were given the opportunity, he would take equally good care of Giff, too. The laugh was on Giff. The poor fool! Her fists clenched. Kirby, Kirby, Kirby! Granted that he was a killer. What of it? This was war, and it demanded blow for blow. He would be the deciding factor. She felt better, stronger, even proud of him. She gloried in his prowess, a curious, fierce pride that she couldn't understand. She who had felt sick to her stomach at the very thought of him now thrilled at the fact that he was their man, her man. She went swiftly to the window, lifted a corner of the starched white curtain and peered out. Kirby and her uncle had their backs turned to her. Her eyes sought and found what they were seeking. The butt of Kirby's big black Colt jutted out of the holster that swung low against his right thigh. He was ready for Giff, ready for anyone who stood before him, Branch or anyone else.

Spanish Joe had felt the overpowering fury of Vance's Colt. Hadn't he fallen before it like wheat before the sweep of a tornado? Could the man Branch hope to withstand him? It was ridiculous. Giff would find that out soon enough. He had failed with Spanish Joe. So, too, would he fail with Branch. Perhaps, in the bitter end, he would take it upon himself to attempt what his hired killers had failed to accomplish. She laughed, as she turned away from the window and set about preparing breakfast.

CHAPTER NINE

GORDON and Lute Bailey were having their mid-morning coffee in the curtained-off back room of their office. It was not a very pretentious setup. There were bare walls on either side of them; a long, gaudy-hued curtain that hung from the ceiling and came to within half an inch of the floor formed a third "wall". Actually its single purpose was to separate the office proper from the lawmen's living quarters. The rear wall contained the back door and a small window that was set unusually high up in the wall. To a critical eye it would have become immediately apparent that both the door and the window had been inserted long after the rear wall had been put up. There was a table in the very middle of the room, a table that tended to slope to the right; there were two cots on opposite sides of the room and three chairs that were now straight-backed, although they had once boasted of armrests. The table was far too big for the room. When anyone wanted to get by, it was necessary to sit down on one of the cots and inch one's way past the overhanging lip of the table and wiggle one's own legs around and past the table's thick legs.

A far corner contained an improvised washstand and a heavy water pitcher. The opposite corner was occupied by an upended box on which a small camp stove had been placed.

The room smelled of many things—cooking, tobacco smoke and a natural mustiness that indicated a need for an airing out. Lute finished drinking his coffee, pushed his cup aside, reached for the third chair and swung it around and hoisted his legs up on it. He sank back in his own chair, his chin on his chest and his hands thrust into his pants pockets. His father looked at him, but he wisely refrained from making any comment.

"Doggone it," Lute finally said explosively.

"What's the matter, Son?"

"Don't anything ever happen around here?"

"Sometimes a sheriff's life become filled to overflowing with excitement," Gordon said. "Fortunately for us nothing's happened so far to require our official attention."

"I could stand some excitement right now," Lute said crossly. "I'm gettin' in my own way."

Gordon Bailey drank his coffee.

"I wish we were back to ranchin', Pop," Lute said. "It gave us somethin' to do. Somethin' worth-while. Besides, we were never so doggoned cramped up like we are here. Ain't enough room to—"

The street door opened and closed.

"Anybody here?" a voice demanded.

Gordon and his son looked at each other.

"I have an idea that the excitement you've been craving has finally arrived," Gordon said. "You'd better find out who's out there."

Lute turned his head.

"Who is it?" he called.

There was no answer; instead they heard a heavy step, then the curtain was whipped back, and they found themselves looking up at a grim-faced Jim Whitaker.

"Oh," Gordon said.

Lute grunted. He swung his legs off the chair, twisted around.

"Somethin' we can do f'r you?" he asked.

Jim Whitaker frowned. "If you think you can spare the time," he said gruffly.

Lute grinned. "Time's the one thing we've got plenty of," he said. "What's on your mind?"

"Your uncle," Jim retorted. "Your father's brother."

Lute's eyebrows arched.

"What about Uncle Giff?" he asked.

"Somebody cut my fence an' ran off some of my stock."

Gordon Bailey looked troubled.

"Which fence?" he asked.

"The one that runs between your property and mine," Jim snapped. "Or what used to be your property."

"And how many steers were run off?"

"All I had in that herd. Hundred an' ninety-two to be exact. What are you going to do about it?"

"We'll look into it for you."

"When?"

"Today."

"What's the matter with now?"

Gordon thought about it for a moment.

"When did you discover the loss of your steers?" he asked.

"First thing this morning," Jim answered. "Look, suppose instead o' wastin' a lot o' time askin' me questions, you get your backside off that chair and into a saddle? I never heard of a lawman catchin' up with a rustler by sittin' in his office. 'Course, if that's askin' or expectin' too much of you—"

The two Baileys arose, interrupting him; they squeezed their way out from under the ledge of the table. Lute's gun belt hung from a nail in the wall above his cot; he reached for it and buckled it around his waist. Gordon had no gun. When he made no attempt to arm himself, Jim eyed him critically.

"Don't you go in for guns?" he asked. "Or did you tote one only when you found an opportunity to take pot shots at the Whitakers?"

Gordon did not answer; he just looked at Jim and smiled.

"All right, Lute," he said. "Let's go."

"You fellers goin' out there now?" Jim asked.

"You want us to investigate the loss of your steers, don't you?" Gordon answered.

Jim's frown deepened. " 'Course," he said gruffly. "Want me to go along?"

"I don't think your presence will be of any help," Gordon said.

Jim Whitaker bristled. "Oh, you don't, hey?"

"No," Gordon said calmly. "However, it's entirely up to you. You can come along, or not. Whichever you choose."

"Come on, Pop," Lute said. "We're on'y wastin' time standin' around jawin' with him."

Jim whirled angrily. "Why, you young—"

"Name calling isn't at all necessary, Whitaker," Gordon said. "I think you can leave this matter in our hands. We'll stop by your place on our way back and let you know what we find."

Lute pushed past Jim. He opened the street door, held it wide, then he followed his father out to the street. The door swung shut behind him. It opened again almost at once, and Jim Whitaker, red-faced and mumbling to himself, came stalking out. He saw the Baileys turn into the alley that led to the rear, but he did not wait for them to return. Instead, he strode across the sidewalk to the kerb, climbed up on his horse and rode swiftly out of town.

Kirby and John Whitaker were just finishing their breakfast when there was a clatter of hoofs. Jane, who was mixing some cake batter at the little work table near the stove, looked up.

"That's him now," John said.

The door opened, and Jim Whitaker came in. He looked angry. He scaled his hat away, came forward to the table, pulled out a chair and seated himself.

"You didn't do so well with the new sheriff," John said. "Huh?"

"No," his brother said.

"I'll have your breakfast in a minute, Dad," Jane said.

"What happened?" John asked.

"I've seen some lawmen in my time," Jim answered. "A lot o' them, too. But that Gordon Bailey ain't even a good imitation o' one."

"What's so surprisin' about that?" John retorted. "Think he'd be any different than he was before, just because somebody pinned a star on him?"

"Dad, what's he going to do about our cattle?" Jane asked.

Jim snorted.

"He an' that worthless son o' his went out to Giff's place

58

to look for th'm," he answered. "They'll stop by here later on an' let us know how they made out."

"H'm," John said, obviously unimpressed.

"H'm is right," Jim said. "They won't find anything. They couldn't find their way home."

"What d'you figger we oughta do?" John asked.

"We won't do anything till after Gordy an' Lute have been here an' gone. Then we'll go lookin' by ourselves. We might find somethin' then."

Jane served her father's breakfast. He attacked it hungrily. She sat down beside him.

"Dad, did you quarrel with Gordon Bailey?" she asked.

"Oh, on'y a little. I had to talk up before he stirred himself. If I hadn'ta, he an' Lute would still be where they were, sittin' on their backsides an' drinkin' coffee. Fine way to hold down a lawman's job awright. Y'know, Jake Holloway put them in there. I hope he never needs 'ny help from them. Because if they don't move 'ny faster f'r him than they did for me, it's gonna be just too bad. He's got one heck uva temper, y'know. He's liable t' pull down the office right smack on their heads. For my dough, they aren't worth their keep in or outta office."

"Once a Bailey, always a Bailey," John said.

"That's right. They don't change, no matter what happens."

Giff Bailey was idling in the doorway of the barn when Gordon and Lute rode up. Giff looked at them and frowned.

"Well?" he demanded. "What are you two doin' out here?"

Lute eased himself in his saddle.

"Giff," Gordon said, "Jim Whitaker came into the office this morning with a complaint. Seems somebody cut his fence and ran off two hundred—"

"Hundred an' ninety-two," Lute said, interrupting him.

"Yes," Gordon said. "One hundred and ninety-two steers."

Giff's mouth tightened. "So what?" he demanded. "What's it got t' do with me?"

"The fence," Gordon said quietly, "separates his property from yours. It's only natural therefore that—"

"He's a damned liar!" Giff yelled. "I didn't have anything t' do with his steers!"

"All right," Gordon said. "I simply told you what

59

brought us out here. We've had a look at the fence and it's cut, just as Whitaker said it was."

"Then he musta done it himself!"

"And he also ran off his own cattle, I suppose?" Gordon asked.

"Them Whitakers are liable t' do anything!"

"We'll have to have a look around, Giff," Gordon said.

"Like hell you will!" Giff yelled. "You get th' hell offa my property an' stay off!"

"Look," Lute said, pointing to the star that was pinned to his shirt front. "We're the law."

"Y'are, hey!" Giff hollered. He jerked out his gun. "This is the on'y law around here! Now both o' you turn around an' get offa this place before I blast you off!"

"Pop," Lute said wearily, "you go back to town. I'm gonna have a look around. You'd better tell Uncle Giff to put away his gun or I'm liable to shove it down his throat. I'll see you later."

He wheeled his horse and rode away. Giff's gun roared and a bullet ploughed the ground and showered Lute's horse's legs with dirt. Lute went on. The gun roared a second time, and the bullet spun into the ground a step ahead of his horse. Lute jerked him to a stop. He wheeled and rode back. Slowly he swung himself out of the saddle. As he started towards Giff, Branch and Coady came up the path from the bunkhouse.

"C'mere, you fellers!" Giff yelled. Lute stopped. Branch and Coady quickened their steps. They came up behind Giff who laughed as he tightened his grip on his gun butt. "Awright, you young pup! Lemme see you do somethin' now!"

"Just a minute," Gordon said. He looked at the two men who had ranged themselves behind his brother, "I'm the sheriff. This young man is my deputy. I'd advise you to think twice before you interfere with the law."

"You get the hell offa my property!" Giff blustered.

"All right," Gordon said calmly. "We will. But we'll be back shortly, with a posse. Come along, Lute."

The youth turned and went back to his horse, climbed up astride him and wheeled. Gordon clattered away. Lute loped after him, overtook him presently and ranged himself alongside.

After they had gone, Giff holstered his gun.

"What was that all about, Boss?" Coady asked.

"The Whitakers claim somebody cut their fence an' ran off some o' their stock," Giff answered.

"Y'mean they're accusin' us o' doin' it?" Coady demanded. "They've got one hell uva nerve!"

Giff trudged into the barn. He came out a minute or two later leading his horse. He climbed into the saddle.

"Goin' to town, Boss?" Coady asked.

"No," Giff replied. "I'm gonna have me a look at that fence."

"Want us t' go along too?"

Giff shook his head. He nudged his horse with his knees, and the animal cantered away.

"You," Coady said, turning quickly to Branch. "Couldn't you have said somethin' like I did to make it look good? You just stood there with your jaw hangin'."

"I don't like the looks o' this business," Branch said.

"This is a hell uva time t' come to that c'nclusion," Coady retorted. "You shoulda thought o' that sooner."

"Maybe I shoulda."

"Aw, f'r Pete's sake, Branch," Coady exclaimed. "What'n blazes is the matter with you anyway, huh? So they're accusin' us o' runnin' off the Whitaker stock. So what? They've gotta prove it before they c'n do anything to us. Now what chance have they got o' doin' that?"

"I dunno," Branch said. "I just wish t' hell we were away from here an' on our way to California."

"Well, just foller my lead," Coady urged, "an' before you know it we'll be headin' for the promised land."

"I sure hope so," Branch said fervently.

"I'm tellin' you. Just keep your shirt on, an' everything'll be awright. I know what I'm talkin' about. I got plans for th' future. I don't aim t' let anything interfere with those plans. Get it?"

CHAPTER TEN

THE pounding of horses' hoofs brought Jim and John Whitaker to their feet.

"That must be Gordy an' young Lute," Jim said. "Come on."

They went to the door, opened it and peered out. Jane wedged her way in between them. Kirby got up from the table and sauntered forward, too; he drew back the curtain and looked out the window. Presently the two Baileys came swinging around the house, pulled up and dismounted. Gordon Bailey strode up to the door, while Lute hung back a bit.

"Well?" Jim Whitaker asked. "How'd you make out?"

"We didn't," Gordon answered.

"Y'mean you didn't find anything?"

"We didn't look," Gordon explained. "We had words with Giff and Lute went for him, but Giff's hired men came along and, when he ordered us off the place, we went."

"I knew I shoulda gone along," Jim said angrily.

"I'm glad you didn't," Gordon said. "It probably would have wound up in a fight, and that wouldn't have served any useful purpose. I told Giff we'd be back with a posse, and that's what we're headed back to town for. I plan to make a thorough search of his place before we look elsewhere."

"H'm," Jim said.

"I'm afraid I'm not a very capable law-enforcement officer," Gordon said. "The job calls for a younger and much more aggressive man than I am. However, I'll see this matter through to the end, then I'll hand in my resignation."

He waited. When no one said anything, he turned and went back to his horse, climbed up into the saddle, wheeled and rode off. Lute swung himself up on his horse effortlessly. He whacked the animal across the rump with his open hand, and the horse snorted protestingly and dashed away.

"I'll be doggoned!" Jim muttered. Evidently he was a bit taken back by Gordon's frankness. "What d'you think o' that? A Bailey admittin' that he ain't all he oughta be!"

"Wonders'll never cease," John said.

"Looks that way."

"What d'you figger t' do? Give Gordy an' his posse a whack at it first, or do you want us to get goin'?"

His brother considered for a moment.

"Y'know, I still can't get over that," he said. "I never thought I'd live t' see the day when a Bailey'd own up to anything. Now I think that since he was man enough to own up to his shortcomings, that maybe we oughta hold off an' kinda give him a chance. What d'you think?"

"It's all right with me," John answered. "I kinda feel the same way you do."

"Then we'll wait till t'night before we go lookin' for ourselves."

"Right."

Jim looked at Kirby, who had just turned away from the window.

"How are you feelin'?" he asked.

"Fine, thank you."

"Have you done any ridin' yet?"

"Oh, yes," Kirby answered quickly. "I've been out twice."

"Bet it felt good t' be on the move again, didn't it?"

Kirby nodded.

"Think you'd like t' trail along with us tonight?"

"Of course. Actually, I had intended going along whether you invited me to or not."

Jim smiled; then he picked up his hat and went out.

"Well," John said. "Think it's about time I got busy, too. What's that cake you're bakin', Janey?"

She turned and smiled.

"Think you'd like chocolate layer cake tonight for a change?" she asked.

"Would I, hey?" he retorted. Then he laughed. "Y'know somethin', Kirby? Ever since she's been feedin' us around here, any time we got peeved at 'er, she'd come up with a choc'lit cake, and that'd be the end of our bein' mad. She's a regular woman. Must be born in th'm to know how to get around men."

The door was pushed open and Jim Whitaker, somewhat out of breath, came rushing back into the house. He kicked the door shut with a backward thrust of his leg.

"S'matter?" John asked quickly.

"Somebody's comin'," Jim replied. "I think it's Giff Bailey."

John Whitaker's eyebrows arched in surprise.

"Giff?" he repeated. "What is this, anyway? Visiting day for the Baileys?"

Now they could hear the swelling clatter of hoofbeats. Quickly they went to the door, opened it and peered out as before. Jane again found room for herself between her father and her uncle. As Kirby came forward to the window, a horseman whirled around the house and jerked his mount to a stiff-legged stop.

"Uh-huh," John Whitaker said out of a corner of his mouth. "Ol' Man Trouble himself."

"Uncle John!" Jane said. "Please!"

Giff looked at them, then he dismounted and came plodding up to the door.

"I didn't come here lookin' for trouble," he announced.

"All right," Jim said. "What did you come here for?"

"About them steers o' yourn."

"Oh," Jim said. "What about th'm?"

"Well, I kinda flew off the handle a little while ago when Gordy an' Lute told me 'bout your fence havin' been cut an' some o' your stock run off your place," Giff explained.

"So we've heard," Jim said dryly.

Giff grinned sheepishly.

"For a minute I thought you sent them over t' my place because you figgered I did it," he continued. "Anyway, after I chased Gordy an' Lute, I went out to see the fence f'r myself."

"Gonna tell me it wasn't cut?"

"Oh, it was cut awright," Giff said quickly. "What's more, I found a lotta tracks across my place."

Jim's eyes brightened. "Y'mean——"

Giff nodded.

"Somebody drove them steers o' yourn across my place," he said. "But where they drove th'm to, that's somethin' I can't answer. Leastways, not yet."

"Mighty decent o' you to come an' tell us that," Jim said.

"On'y did it because I didn't want you t' think I went in f'r cattle rustlin'," Giff said quickly. "I draw th' lines somewheres, y'know."

"Giff, you got 'ny idea who it coulda been?"

"I got'n idea, sure. But since it's on'y an idea, I ain't sayin' yet. I've got my own ways o' gettin' to the bottom o' things. So don't try t' pin me down on who I think it was till I kinda check up on a couple o' things. Soon's I know, I'll see to it that you do, too. Awright?"

"Yeah, sure. But look, Giff, in case you need 'ny help . . ."

Giff grinned again, "Yeah?"

"Well, doggone it—holler an' we'll come a-runnin'."

Giff hitched up his pants.

"Gotta get back t' my place," he said. He shifted his holster a bit. "Oh, yeah! Now just because I came over here peaceable, don't go thinkin' I'm gettin' soft. Soon's this is over, I'll start hatin' you Whitakers same as I always did an' always will."

" 'Course!"

"I still think that stream is just as much mine as it is yourn an' nobody, not even all the courts in the world, can ever make me think different. That clear?"

"Clear enough," Jim said with a grin.

Giff cocked his head; he eyed Jane for a moment.

"That's your daughter, eh?" he said. "Not bad-lookin'. Just her hard luck that she was born a Whitaker."

"Indeed!" Jane said icily. "Imagine if I had been born a Bailey!"

Giff frowned darkly.

"Don't you gimme any o' your sass, young un," he said gruffly. "It's bad enough I gotta hear it from that young squirt, Lute. The two uv you need a good hair brushin' to teach you somethin'."

He turned on his heel and went striding back to his horse, climbed up on him, wheeled and loped off.

Jim and John Whitaker looked at each other.

"Well?" Jim asked.

"Well what?" John asked.

"What d'you make o' this business?"

"I dunno. It just seems t' me that there's somethin' rotten 'round these parts."

"What do you mean?"

"Well, who d'you think he thinks did this thing?"

"Branch?"

" 'Course. There ain't anybody else. It just has t' be Branch. That is, if Giff's tellin' the truth."

"I kinda think he is."

"Yeah, I suppose so. But where does that leave us?"

"We're still goin' ridin' tonight."

"I think we oughta."

When Coady came out of the bunkhouse, there was no sign of Branch. When he heard a hammering sound, he looked around quickly.

"Hey, Branch!" he yelled. "Where are you?"

"In the barn!"

Coady strode up the path, halted in the doorway of the barn and peered in.

"What are you doin'?" he asked.

"Fixin' up these stalls."

"What d'you do? Look for things to do?"

"I like keepin' myself busy," Branch answered. "Helps keep me fr'm thinkin' too much."

Coady shook his head.

"Y'know, I wouldn't have t' know anything about you, yet I could tell damned quick that you'd been up to somethin'. You act about as guilty as all hell."

"Maybe it'd look a lot better if you did somethin' around here, too."

"I on'y do what I hafta," Coady said sharply. "It don't get you anywhere, workin' all the time."

"Don't it?" Branch asked with a grin. "How d'you know? You ever try it?"

"'Course I did," Coady fired back. "When I was young an' didn't know any better. I used t' wonder why it was that the fellers who hustled fr'm morning to night were always the first ones t' be fired when things got tough, while the ones who just seemed t' lay around on their fannies were kept on."

"Yeah, and what did you find out?"

"That you're a sucker if you knock y'self out for any boss. And that holds good f'r Bailey, too."

"Hey, ain't it funny that he hasn't come back yet?"

"Oh, I dunno. Maybe he went somewheres else, too, besides ridin' out to see that fence. Anyway, what's the difference? Don't tell me you're lonesome for 'im?"

Branch laughed.

"Not exactly," he said, then he grew grave again. "You don't think he—"

"Found out anything?"

Branch nodded. Coady frowned.

"You better go on hammerin'," he said. He shook his head again. "You're just about the doggonedest feller I ever knew. You always been like that?"

"Like what?"

"The kind that always worries about somethin'?"

"Only when I've had somethin' to worry about," Branch said.

Coady turned on his heel and trudged off to the corral. He climbed up and seated himself on the top rail. He had just made himself comfortable when he heard a clatter of hoofs. He twisted around. A horseman came pounding into view. It was Giff Bailey. Coady eyed him, watched him ride past the bunkhouse and saw him pull up in front of the barn. Giff dismounted and led his horse inside. Branch was on his knees, driving a nail into a stall board. Giff watched him for a moment.

"What are you doin'?" Giff asked.

Branch turned his head.

"Oh," he said. "Didn't hear you come in."

"What are you doin' there?"

"These stalls are fallin' apart," Branch explained. "So I fixed th'm up."

Giff grunted.

"Where's Coady?" he asked.

"Oh, somewheres around. Want 'im?"

"No. Wait a minute. . . . Yeah, call him."

Branch got up, went to the doorway. He spied Coady sitting on the corral rail.

"Coady!" he yelled. When Coady turned and looked at him, Branch beckoned. "Boss wants you!"

Giff unsaddled his horse. He turned his head when Coady strode into the barn.

"Want me, Boss?"

"Yeah. I was gonna have Branch go an' do it, but since he's got somethin' to do, you c'n go. Get some wire outta the tool shed and ride out an' fix up that busted fence before any more Whitaker stock gets lost. Don't leave the busted pieces o' wire hangin' there. Cut th'm off."

"What'll I cut th'm with?"

"With a wire cutter of course. There used t' be one in the tool shed. See if it's still there."

"It's gone, Boss," Branch called. "I cleaned up the tool shed just the other day, an' there wasn't any wire cutter around that I could see."

Giff looked annoyed.

"Wait a minute," Branch said, coming forward. "Coady's got a cutter. I just remembered."

Giff's head jerked around in Coady's direction.

"You're locoed," Coady said calmly. "I've never owned a wire cutter in my life."

"Oh," Branch said. "Guess I was mistaken."

He looked from Coady to Giff, then he turned away suddenly and strode back to the rear.

There was a brief, hushed silence.

"Forget it for t'day," Giff said finally. "T'morrow when I go to town I'll get a new cutter, then you c'n string up some wire an' help keep the Whitaker stock on their side o' the fence."

He marched out of the barn, tramped up the path to the house. There was a strange expression on his face. His hand tightened around the butt of his gun.

CHAPTER ELEVEN

MEALTIME in Giff Bailey's house was never completely devoted to eating. If no one else had anything to talk about, Giff could always be counted upon to provide a topic for conversation, and a good deal of the discussion. When the conversation seemed to be lagging, Giff took command of it. He talked freely. He was not one to withhold his opinion when he felt inclined to voice it. He had his own views on every subject, and he never took a middle course; he was either for or against, and he never left any doubt in his listeners' minds as to where he stood.

However, this suppertime there was no conversation, and Giff was unusually quiet. As a matter of fact, he was not only tight-lipped but grim-faced as well. When he had finished eating, he pushed his plate away, sat back in his chair and looked first at Coady, then at Branch.

"You fellers are awf'lly quiet tonight," he remarked. He eyed them closely. "S'matter? You both all talked out?"

Branch did not look up; but Coady did, as calmly and casually as ever; he even flashed a smile.

"Every day, in fact at every meal we've had since you came here, Coady," Giff went on presently, "we've heard nothing but Texas and how wonderful it is. Don't tell me you've run outta stuff to tell us about Texas? Here I am just about sold on Texas and almost ready to brag about it like I came from there, too, and you sit there without a word to say. It's kinda discouraging. Makes me wonder if you haven't been dreamin' up that stuff."

"Nope," Coady said. "Texas is everything I've said it is, and then some."

Giff grunted.

"I'm glad to hear you say that," he said. "Kinda relieves my mind. But how come you're so clammed up tonight? You off your feed, or is it that redheaded woman down at the Oasis?"

Coady smiled again.

"Neither one," he replied.

"And you, Branch," Giff said, turning to him again. "You ain't much of a talker ord'narily, so I don't expect too much gab outta you. But tonight you're quieter than ever. You're closed up tighter'n a drum. You haven't looked up even once since you started to eat. What's the matter with you?"

"Nothing," Branch answered, raising his eyes and promptly lowering them again.

"Don't gimme that," Giff scoffed. "Somethin's botherin' you. I c'n tell. You and Coady have a fallin' out?"

" 'Course not," Coady said.

"I asked him," Giff snapped. "Not you."

"We get along awright," Branch said.

"There y'are," Coady said.

Giff ignored him. He fixed his eyes on Branch.

"Y'mean you got your full share o' the dough without havin' to fight for it?" he asked.

Branch's head jerked, but he managed to check it and held it stiffly. His ears suddenly reddened.

"S'matter?" Giff asked. "Did I surprise you by askin' you that? You didn't think you could pull anything around here without me gettin' wind of it, did you? If you did, then you fellers've got an awful lot to learn. Who'd you sell the Whitaker stock to?"

Coady laughed, and Branch's head jerked up again. The blood had drained out of his face giving him a greyish, ashen colour. He stared at Coady with widened eyes. There was fear in them.

"You don't have to tell me if you don't want to," Giff went on gruffly. "I'll find out soon enough."

"Boss," Coady said, and Giff looked at him. "What makes you think we had anything to do with those steers?"

Giff's lips whipped back in a smile, a knowing smile.

"I know you had everything to do with th'm," he answered. "What I don't know is—did you get a decent price for th'm?"

Branch's eyes shuttled from one to the other.

"You tell us, Boss," Coady said brazenly. "You seem to know more about this than we do."

"Gonna try to bluff your way right through to the end, huh?" Giff said. He shrugged his thick shoulders. "It's awright with me. It's your funeral, not mine. All I hope is that you fellers had better sense than to do business with that Les Gillen. If you didn't, then it's gonna be just too bad. I wouldn't trust that maverick any further'n I could throw him, and believe me, that ain't far. One o' these days the law's gonna catch up with Mister Gillen. When they put the pressure on him he'll spill his guts, and you know where you'll be then. Right smack up the creek."

"Go on, Boss," Coady urged. "Keep talkin'. This is gettin' more interesting all the time."

Giff shook his head. "Nope," he said with finality. "That's all there is. There isn't any more. Only remember, the next time you decide to run off somebody's cattle, pick a better spot for it, and be kinda choosey 'bout who you do business with."

Coady was thoughtfully silent for a moment. Then he folded his arms on the table and leaned a bit towards Giff.

"Y'know," he said quietly, "we did make a mistake at that. But it was all my doin', not Branch's."

Giff's eyebrows arched. "That so?"

"Yep," Coady said, nodding. "I can see it now awright, and I know I should've seen it right off. We should've counted you in on the deal right from the start instead o' wisin' up after it was done and over with. You're smart, Boss. A heaper smarter, I'll bet, than anybody gives you credit for being."

"G'wan," Giff said expansively. "You're just pullin' my leg."

"I am, huh?" Coady retorted. "Just to prove to you that I'm not, suppose I tell you that we're countin' you in on the deal, and that we're splittin' the five thousand bucks we got three ways?" He paused for a moment, deliberately, then he went on again, "You're probably a heap better at figgers than we are. How much does it come to for each of us, splittin' the five thousand in three? About seventeen hundred apiece?"

"Closer to sixteen hundred and sixty-five," Giff said.

"Uh-huh," Coady said. "Cuttin' you in gives us a little less than we figgered, I mean Branch an' me, but it's awright with me. How 'bout it, Branch?"

"Yeah, sure," Branch said eagerly. "It's awright with me."

"But it ain't awright with me," Giff said quietly.

The other two men looked at him.

"Huh?" Coady asked. "What d'you mean?"

"I mean that you're a couple o' no good so-an'sos," Giff said harshly. "I don't want any o' that dough. I've been mean and ornery and just about everything else in the book. But I've never taken anything that wasn't mine, and I don't aim to start doin' it now."

"I see," Coady said slowly. He moved back into his

chair. "You were just leadin' us on, gettin' us to spill everything."

"I just wanted to show you fellers you aren't as smart as you think you are, 'specially you, Coady," Giff said sharply. "You're not even fair to middlin' at bein' crooked."

Branch's eyes were again shuttling from one to the other.

There was a brief silence. It was Coady who shattered it by shifting in his chair.

"Guess you don't want us around here any longer," he said presently.

"You're damned right I don't!" Giff shot back.

"And the minute we pull out you're gonna get word to the law," Coady said in a curious, musing tone. "Aren't you?"

"What I'm gonna do," Giff said curtly, "is my business."

Coady smiled deeply. Then he shook his head. "That's where you're wrong, Bailey," he said quietly. "Dead wrong."

"That so?"

"Sure. It's so important to us, I mean what you do, that we've just naturally gotta make it our business too."

Giff Bailey did not answer; he frowned, but he held his tongue.

"You shouldn't have tricked us like that," Coady said. "We thought you were with us, an' we came clean with you, an' you let us down."

There was a deep silence again; it hung over them like a pall.

Finally, Coady sighed. "I'm afraid we can't afford to take any more chances with you, Bailey," he said. "It wouldn't be safe for us. Y'know?"

His right arm jerked suddenly. There was a deafening roar that seemed to shake the building to its very foundation. Giff gasped painfully as though the breath had been driven out of his body. Gun smoke began to curl upward from beneath the ledge of the table. Until that second Giff hadn't moved. Then suddenly he leaned forward against the table. He sagged brokenly, and slipped sideways. His chair tipped with his weight and crashed with him to the floor. Branch's wide eyes followed Giff; he stared at the hunched-up body, then he slowly turned his head and raised his eyes to meet Coady's. His face was white.

Coady looked at him and shook his head.

"I hated to do that," he said. "But I had to. I didn't have 'ny choice."

Branch nodded understandingly. "I know," he said. "But I still wish you hadn'ta done it."

"It's too late for that now. It's done."

"Yeah," Branch said heavily.

"You better go saddle up for both of us," Coady directed. "They tell me it's a helluva long ride to California. The sooner we start, the sooner we'll get there."

Branch arose slowly; Coady watched him.

"Y'know," Coady said, and Branch turned to him again. "You worry me, too. Those long years in prison did somethin' to you. Took somethin' outta you. It's hard for me to b'lieve that you once killed a ranger. If you had guts once, you haven't got 'em any more."

Branch opened his mouth to answer; he reconsidered, evidently, for he closed his mouth again almost at once.

"Y'see?" Coady said. "You clam up when you should say something, and when you oughtn'ta open your mouth you get gabby and talk outta turn. That's bad."

Coady's gun came up on the table. He studied the big Colt with its blackened muzzle.

"Now take that business about the wire cutter," he said without looking up. "You sure talked outta turn then."

"I know," Branch admitted lamely. "I coulda kicked myself afterward."

"I think that's what gave us away to Bailey," Coady went on. "Y'know that, Branch?"

"It won't happen again. I'll watch myself and make sure."

"But suppose you forget, Al, and it does happen again? Where'll we be then?"

"I won't forget, I tell you," Branch said doggedly.

Coady raised his eyes. "I wish I could be sure o' that," he said.

"I'm tellin' you I'll watch myself."

Coady was silent now. It was apparent to Branch that he was not convinced.

"Look," Branch said, "maybe you'll feel safer if you go off by yourself. Then you won't have to worry none 'bout me talkin' outta turn or not talkin' up when you think I oughta."

"Yeah," Coady mused thoughtfully. "Maybe that would be the best way after all."

"If that's the way you want it."

"You won't be sore about it though, will you?"

"Nope."

"Or disappointed?"

Branch shrugged. "You've got the right to go the way you want," he said. "Same's I have to go the way I want."

"I'm glad you're takin' it like that, Al."

"Ain't any sense takin' it any other way," Branch said. "Want me to go first?"

"Yeah. D'you mind?"

"First or last, it's all the same to me."

Coady shifted the gun to his left hand. He arose and held out his right hand.

"So long, Al," he said, and he smiled.

Branch gripped hands with him.

"So long," he said.

They parted, and Branch hitched up his pants and started towards the door.

"Al," Coady called, and Branch stopped and looked back at him over his shoulder. "Al, you don't aim to head for town and tell the law 'bout Bailey, do you?"

Branch looked surprised. " 'Course not," he replied. "What gave you that idea?"

"I dunno. It just came to me, and it made me wonder."

Branch looked at him obliquely.

"You don't trust anybody," he said after a moment; "do you?"

Coady laughed. "To tell you the truth, Al," he said. "No."

Branch shook his head. He turned away and reached for the doorknob. His hand tightened around it as Coady's gun thundered. Branch gasped and fell against the door. Coady, his gun raised and ready, came around the table. He halted and watched Branch force himself up again; he backed a bit as Branch turned towards him. When Branch took a stumbling step forward, Coady again gave ground before him.

"You dirty—dirty . . ." Branch wheezed with a chest-heaving effort to get his breath.

The Colt roared again spitefully, drowning out the panting, weakened voice, and Branch clutched his middle with his big hands and tottered brokenly. He swayed drunkenly, then he stiffened, rising to his full height; when he attained it, he suddenly pitched forward. Coady, on the alert, side-stepped nimbly, and Branch toppled past him like a felled

73

tree, struck on his face with his brawny arms outflung. Coady looked down at him and nudged him with his boot toe; when Branch did not move, Coady holstered his gun and bent over him and put his hand in Branch's pants pocket. When he came erect again he had a roll of bills in his hand. He thrust the roll into his shirt, then without a glance at Branch or Bailey, he went striding out of the house.

He returned a minute later and turned out the light in the swinging ceiling lamp, plunging the room into total, gloomy darkness. There was a quick step, and the door closed quietly as Coady went out. His boots crunched briefly on the path that led to the barn; the sound faded out shortly and a heavy silence deepened over the place. There was a snort, the hollow step of iron-shod hoofs on the barn's wooden flooring, the creak of sweat-stiffened saddle leather, the explosive crack of reins as the horse was whipped into motion, a flurry of hoofs that swelled and died out in almost the same moment; then Coady was gone, and the silence returned and settled itself again.

It was probably an hour later when three shadowy horsemen appeared and jogged past the corral and the bunkhouse and pulled up when they came abreast of the barn.

"Not a single light showin' anywhere," Jim Whitaker said, easing himself in the saddle and looking about him. "Wonder if they've turned in already?"

"The corral's empty," John Whitaker said beside him. "If they've turned in, then their horses oughta be in the barn."

"I'll have a look," Jim said. He dismounted, trudged over to the barn, halted in the doorway and peered in. A match flamed into light in his cupped hand, and he went inside. He came out again shortly. "Two horses in there."

"Should be three o' them," John said.

"Should be, yeah," his brother retorted. "Only there ain't."

"Means that somebody hasn't turned in yet. Probably Giff himself."

"How about going right up to the house?" Kirby, the third horseman, asked.

"Yeah," Jim said. "That's better than guessing. Come on."

He climbed up on his horse and led the way up the path to the back door, then he dismounted again and knocked.

74

There was no response. He rapped a second time, then a third time, moved to the window and peered in.

"See anything?" John asked.

"Nope. Nothing."

"Door locked?"

"Dunno," Jim answered over his shoulder. "Haven't tried it yet."

"Why don't you?"

"I aim to," Jim retorted grumpily.

He retraced his steps to the door. He turned the knob and the door opened.

"Open, huh?" John said. "That's funny."

He swung himself off his horse. Kirby climbed down, too. They joined Jim in the doorway, crowded around him.

"Somebody got a match?" the latter asked. "The one I used up in the barn must've been the only one I had on me."

John dug in his pockets; he produced a couple from each coat pocket.

"Here y'are," he said. "Here's four o' th'm."

Jim took them. He scratched one on his pants leg, and yellow flame sputtered against the background of night darkness.

"See anything?" John asked, peering hard over his brother's shoulder.

The flame sputtered and went out; John grumbled, and Jim cursed under his breath. Kirby stepped around Jim and pushed forward into the kitchen.

"Here's somebody," he called from the darkness beyond the doorway.

Jim lit another match.

"Huh?" he asked. "Who is it?"

When John crowded past him into the kitchen, Jim stepped inside, too. The brothers gathered around Kirby, who was turning Branch over on his back.

"Hey," John said in excited tones. "Is that—Giff?"

Holding the match carefully, Jim bent over Branch.

"Nope," he said. "That ain't Giff. Ain't anything like him either. This feller's bigger and younger."

John bent over Branch. He studied the dead man's face.

"Nope," he said, straightening up. "He ain't anybody I've ever seen before."

The second match began to flicker out.

"How 'bout lighting that ceiling lamp?" Kirby asked, pointing to it.

Jim Whitaker stepped around him. He lit another match from the one that was beginning to die and curl in his hand; when the fresh one flamed, he dropped the burned-out stick on the floor. Presently bright light filled the room.

"Hey, Jim," John said suddenly. "Think this might be that Branch feller?"

Jim shrugged his shoulders. "Dunno," he answered. He stood over Branch again. "It's a long time, y'know, since I saw Branch last, and he coulda changed a lot."

"Maybe this is the other fellow," Kirby suggested. "The fellow from Texas."

"Nope," John said, shaking his head. "Seems to me Hanley said Branch was big and heavy and thick through the shoulders. Then somebody else, I think it was Jake Holloway, said the other feller, Coady, was tall and lean. Built something like you, Kirby."

"Then this must be Branch," Kirby said. "He's a pretty big fellow, deep-chested and broad-shouldered."

"Yeah," Jim said. "Guess this is him, all right."

"Or was," John added dryly. "He's dead as he'll ever be."

John moved away. He stopped in front of the table.

"Three places set," he said in a musing tone. He turned around. "Jim, you don't suppose Giff and Coady could've plugged Branch and then cleared out, do you?"

"They could've, sure," Jim answered. "But it doesn't make sense."

"No-o, I suppose it doesn't," John admitted. "But whoever heard of a killing that made sense, huh?"

He moved around the table. He stopped abruptly and bent his head.

"Here's another one!" he said excitedly. "Layin' under the table!"

Kirby and Jim Whitaker came to his side at once. They stared at the huddled body that lay on the floor against the leg of the table. Kirby moved towards it, caught up the chair that had tipped over and crashed with Giff Bailey and slung it away.

"That's Giff," Jim breathed.

The brothers bent over the dead rancher.

"If this is Giff Bailey," Kirby said, and they looked up at him, "and the other fellow is Branch, then it narrows down to Coady."

"Uh-huh," John said, straightening up again. "Now all

76

we've gotta do is find Coady, and the mystery o' what happened here will be solved."

Jim arose and sauntered thoughtfully to the open door.

"Come on," he said, turning in the doorway. "We'd better get a posse out after Coady before he gets too far away. John, turn out that light. Kirby, if you don't feel up to doin' any more ridin' around tonight, you go back to the house."

"I'd like to look around a bit first," Kirby said as he came across the room.

"That's up to you," Jim responded. "Only I don't think you oughta push y'self too much yet."

The ceiling light went out, and the three men trooped out of the house. Jim and Kirby went at once to their horses and climbed up on them; John closed the door behind him and mounted and wheeled away with the others.

"Well," Jim said when they rode around the house, "this is where we leave you, Kirby. We'll see you later."

"Right."

"Watch y'self," John added.

The brothers rode away. Kirby settled himself in the saddle and nudged his horse with his knees and headed for the fence that separated the Whitaker and Bailey ranches.

CHAPTER TWELVE

It was Kirby's intention to ride the Bailey spread from wire to wire, beginning with the western fence, the dividing line between the two properties. Accordingly, he followed it southward, taking note, as he came abreast of it, of the break-through, the point at which the fence had been cut to permit the rustlers to reach and corral the immediately accessible Whitaker steers and herd them through on to Bailey property and drive them across it to their destination. He knew it would be futile in the night light to attempt to pick up and follow the tracks of the stolen cattle; he sought something more tangible, something that would be immediately recognizable as Whitaker property, an injured steer that had been trampled and abandoned, or an unruly one that had been cut adrift, or even the body of a dead steer. He admitted he was asking a lot, but he sought it anyway, and hoped he would find it.

When he·reached the end of the strung line, he wheeled and loped along the southern boundary, and followed it towards its juncture with the eastern fence. He had already noticed that the ground was becoming increasingly rough, even a bit hilly in spots. Sun-bleached, white-faced boulders of varying shapes and sizes loomed up, studding the south-eastern corner, and gleaming with an eerie brightness against the night. There were rock formations close by, too, and the smell of denned-up snakes was in the air. He checked his mount, slowed him to a walk as they neared the corner. They went on, despite his horse's nasally voiced protests, threading their way among the boulders. The animal's iron-shod hoofs trod shale with a grinding, crunching sound; each hoofbeat rang out clearly upon the few stony stretches and filled the air with an echoing metallic clatter.

"Hold it!" a voice suddenly called out. Kirby jerked his startled horse to an abrupt stop and sat quietly astride him, disregarding his impatient pawing of the ground. "Get your hands up and keep th'm up!"

Kirby obeyed without protest or delay. He raised his hands and waited. Although there was opportunity for a stealthy glance behind him, he did not take advantage of. it. He heard a scraping sound near by, the sound of a booted man scrambling or sliding down from the rocks. He gave brief consideration to snatching his gun from his holster and shooting his way to freedom before his approaching captor was fully prepared for such a move, but he rejected the idea. He had already decided that the man was Coady; if so, he was willing to chance anything in return for an opportunity to turn the tables on Coady and capture him.

Coady, he reasoned, had sought to make his escape southward. Just what had delayed him, or why he was still lingering on the Bailey place, Kirby couldn't explain. However, the Texan had probably heard him coming and, thinking himself overtaken by a posse, had hastily taken refuge in the rocks.

Now there was an approaching step and presently the man came up to Kirby and stopped within a few feet of him.

"Awright," he said authoritatively. "What's your name and what are you doin' around here?"

The voice was surprisingly youthful. It couldn't be Coady's, Kirby decided. He had been expecting a mature drawl.

"My name's Kirby," he replied. "I'm just riding around."

"Kirby, hey?" the man repeated. There was surprise in his voice. He came closer, a husky, shadowy figure with a half-raised rifle gripped in his hands. Moonlight ran along the barrel of the rifle. He looked up at Kirby. "Take off your hat," he commanded and gestured with his rifle, "and raise your head so's I can get a good look at you."

Again Kirby obeyed. The man studied him for a moment, grunted and lowered his rifle.

"Awright," he said. "That's all."

"Thanks," Kirby said dryly. He put on his hat and turned a bit in the saddle. "You're a Bailey, aren't you?"

"That's right. Lute Bailey. But how'd you know?"

"Recognized something in your voice. Is your father here with you?"

"Nope," Lute answered. "Why? You want him for somethin'?"

"Just to tell him that his brother's dead."

"Huh?" Lute said, plainly jolted. "Y'mean—Uncle Giff?"

"Yes."

Lute stared hard at him. It was apparent that he found Kirby's news hard to believe.

"What d'you mean dead?" he demanded. "Y'mean somebody killed him?"

"That's right."

"How d'you know about it? Somebody tell you?"

"No," Kirby answered. "The Whitakers and I stopped to see him earlier this evening. We found him dead on his kitchen floor. He'd been shot."

"I'll be doggoned!"

"He lay behind the table," Kirby continued, "and one of his men, Branch, I think, lay midway between the table and the door. Maybe just a little closer to the table than the door."

"Go on," Lute commanded. "What about the other feller?"

"Coady?"

"Yeah, that's the one. Tall feller. What about him? Wasn't he around?"

"There wasn't any sign of him," Kirby replied. "His horse wasn't in the barn either."

"Uh-huh," Lute said thoughtfully. "Y'think he did it?"

"It looks that way."

Lute was silent for a minute.

"Where are the Whitakers now?" he asked.

"They're rounding up a posse to run down Coady."

"Pop's out with a posse now," Lute said. "I wish he'd come back so's I could tell him about Uncle Giff."

"What are you doing out here?" Kirby asked. "Scouting around on your own hook?"

"I was plannin' to," Lute answered. Then his tone changed and his voice reflected his disgust. "Pop told me to stay put here till he gets back. Got an idea somebody might come bustin' through the pass. That's a laugh. Nobody ever uses the pass. Outside o' you, I haven't seen even a shadow. What's more, I don't expect to see any."

"What's your idea, Lute?"

"What d'you mean?"

"What do you think happened to the Whitakers' cattle?"

"They were run off, of course," Lute said promptly.

"Yes, but where were they run off to? Don't you think they're still somewhere around here?"

"Nope," the husky youth said firmly. "Uncle Giff was ornery, awright, but he was honest. He didn't want anything that wasn't his. What's more, he wouldn't stand for any o' his hands runnin' off somebody else's stock and hidin' th'm away on his place. I rode around it yesterday and I looked everywhere, but there wasn't a single sign o' th'm. The Whitakers ever mention a rancher named Gillen? Les Gillen?"

"I don't think so. The name doesn't sound at all familiar."

Kirby eased himself in the saddle.

"This Gillen owns a pretty good-sized spread just the other side o' the pass," Lute told him, nodding southward. "Accordin' to what I've heard tell of him, Mister Gillen goes in for anything that'll make him a buck, and he ain't the least bit fussy 'bout what it is."

"And you think Gillen has the Whitakers' cattle. Is that what you're trying to tell me?"

"Yep," Lute said with finality.

"Perhaps we ought to go see Mister Gillen," Kirby said. "If not directly, perhaps we might have a look around his place."

"I think the last part o' that would be the smartest,"

Lute said. "He's supposed to have some real tough characters workin' for him."

"Well? What are we waiting for?"

"For Pop. Soon's he gets back we can get goin'."

"We don't want to lose too much time, you know."

"Suppose we give Pop say half 'n hour, huh? If he doesn't show up by then we'll go anyway. Awright?"

"Half an hour you said."

"And half 'n hour is what I mean," Lute said. He pushed his hat up from his eyes. "Like to ask you somethin', Kirby."

"All right. What is it?"

"It's about Janey. You know, Jane Whitaker."

"Oh," Kirby said. "So that's really what's on your mind!"

"Yep. You like her?"

"Very much. I imagine everyone else does too. Don't you like her?"

"Hey, I'm the one who's askin' the questions. Remember?"

Kirby laughed. "I'm sorry," he said. "Go ahead."

"Does she like you?"

"I'm afraid I can't answer that."

"Why not?" Lute demanded.

"Simply because she has never told me."

Lute stared at him again.

"Heck, do you have to be told when a girl likes you? Don't you know? Can't you tell?"

"I'm afraid you don't understand, Lute."

"I'd sure like to," Lute retorted. "Janey's cute and pretty and smart as all get-out, and on top o' that she's got plenty o' guts. Nobody's ever gonna walk over her."

"I think I'll go along with everything you've said about her so far."

"Then what in blazes d'you want?"

"I don't want anything."

"Well, you wanna marry her, don't you?"

"No."

"Huh?" Lute said, somewhat taken back. "How come you don't wanna marry her?"

"I have a wife already."

"Huh?" Lute said, jolted for the second time. "You have?"

"Yes. And just for the record, Jane knows that. I told her."

"I'll be doggoned!" Lute said, and he laughed. "I'm sure glad to hear that. Believe me!"

"I take it, Lute, you're somewhat interested in Jane yourself."

"You take it right! Say, Kirby, she ever say anything about me?"

"I don't believe so."

"Oh," Lute said.

There was unconcealed disappointment in his voice, and something of a letdown in his bearing.

"On the other hand," Kirby added quickly, "she may have spoken of you any number of times, and I may have forgotten. Either way though, it doesn't mean anything, and I wouldn't give it a second thought if I were you."

"Uh-huh," Lute said, brightening a bit. "Some girls mightn't talk about those things. Y'know? They might keep them to th'mselves."

"Of course. And Jane is probably that kind."

"Kirby, y'think I'd have a chance with her?"

"Don't you think you should ask her that yourself?"

"I aim to," Lute said quickly. "And doggoned soon, too!"

"That's the idea!"

"Hey, y'know something? I'm glad this happened. I mean you comin' along and me stoppin' you and us gettin' a chance to talk like we've been doin'."

Kirby smiled.

"Look," Lute said. "I want you to know I wasn't the one who plugged you. As a matter o' fact, tryin' to find out who it was that did is what Uncle Giff and I had that fight about. Leastways, that's what led to the fight."

"Wait a minute now. You mean it was your uncle who shot me?"

"I didn't say that. Anyway, Uncle Giff is dead. So let's forget it."

"We-ll," Kirby began a bit reluctantly. Then he gestured, indicating that he was willing to dismiss the subject. "All right, Lute. We'll forget about it. But don't you think we've waited long enough for your father to return?"

Lute considered briefly.

"Y'think it's more'n the half 'n hour we said we'd give him?" he asked.

"If it isn't, it must be pretty close to it."

"Then we won't wait any longer."

"Where's your horse?"

"Down a ways behind some boulders," Lute answered. "Won't take me more'n a minute to get him."

"I'll wait for you."

Lute hurried away. He disappeared from sight shortly. Then about a minute or two later, there was the sound of hoofs on the hard ground, and Lute rode into view again, outlined by the moonlight.

"Come on," he called.

Kirby wheeled his mount and rode towards him.

"I'll take the lead," Lute said.

"Right," Kirby responded. "But don't get too far ahead of me."

Lute rode off, and Kirby, quickening his horse's pace, pulled into position directly behind him. The sharp metallic clatter of their horses' hoofs rang in the air. For a moment it swelled, then suddenly, as they encountered and jogged over a stretch of grassy ground, it faded out.

Lute twisted around. "The pass," he called. "We're coming to it."

Kirby did not answer; there was no need to. The ground was barren again, and suddenly there were walls on both sides of them; short walls at first, then they were shoulder-high, and finally, they were tall, raggedy-edged walls that towered high above them. The hoofbeats rang out even louder now; in fact, the echo seemed to linger longer, too, due no doubt to the confining walls which served as sounding boards. A couple of times Lute turned his head and looked back; each time Kirby gave him an assuring wave of his hand, and they went on. Minutes passed, minutes that seemed unusually long and unending; finally the walls began to taper off and they emerged into the open. Lute drew rein and waited till Kirby came up alongside him.

"Gillen's layout begins here," Lute said. "Y'wanna watch yourself from here on. The ground slopes downward, kinda sharp too in some places, and 'less you're set for it, you're liable to find your horse takin' the downgrade on his backside instead of his feet."

Kirby smiled. However, he tightened his grip on the reins, and they were on the move again. The ground, just as Lute had cautioned him, was suddenly sharply downhill. Once or twice Kirby's horse lost his footing on the grassy slope and started to slide; each time, though, Kirby, who was watching alertly, managed to pull him to an abrupt stop. There was a moment's wait each time; then when the horse offered no protest to Kirby's urging, they went on. They reached the bottom of the incline finally, and Lute pulled up again.

"From here on," he said, "it's pretty even ground. There are a couple o' small dips here and there, and a couple o' rises to match them, but they aren't anything to worry about. We'll take th'm as we come to th'm."

"Wait a minute now," Kirby said, looking about him. "There's something here that puzzles me, and the more I think about it the more it makes me wonder if we aren't chasing a rainbow."

"What d'you mean?"

Kirby turned to him again. "Well, frankly, Lute, I'm wondering if we aren't after the wrong man."

Lute looked at him blankly.

"What I mean is this," Kirby said patiently. "If Gillen's outfit really ran off the Whitaker stock, doesn't it seem odd to you that they haven't taken any precautions to prevent or guard against a surprise visit by the law, or even the Whitakers?"

"Oh," Lute said. "I've been wondering about the same thing. I kinda expected we'd run into some o' his hired hands once we got through the pass."

"Willing to admit you've guessed wrong about Gillen this time?"

"Nope," the youth answered calmly. "I still think Gillen's our man."

"Then why in thunder isn't he concerned about leaving his place wide open to anyone who wants to see what he's doing?" Kirby demanded. "If he had anything to hide, he'd have guards posted, wouldn't he, to keep people out?"

"Take it easy now," Lute said with a grin. "There are two ways o' figgerin' this out. First, Gillen's a shipper. He's always buyin' and shippin' out cattle. That's his business. It could be he's got all his hands busy with a shipment."

"All right," Kirby conceded. "What's the second way?"

"Gillen's smart, cute. I wouldn't put it past him to let us get this far or even a piece farther into his place before he jumps us."

"H'm," Kirby said thoughtfully. "How does he ship? By railroad?"

"Nope. By water."

"You mean there's a river close by here?"

"Sure. If we were to keep ridin' straight ahead for maybe six or eight miles, we'd hit it head on. See what he does, Kirby? He drives his steers straight down to the river, loads them on flatboats and—"

"I see!"

"Lemme finish. Anyway, that's the cheapest way o' shipping. He floats th'm down the river, and somewheres along the line somebody meets him and takes over for him. This somebody must own the boats and must bring them up the river whenever Gillen sends him word he's got somethin' for him."

"But before Gillen can ship out, he's got to alter the brands on the cattle he hasn't really bought."

"Changin' a brand is called venting."

"Thanks."

"You're welcome," Lute said with a grin. "Anyway, what you're drivin' at is that the feller down the river doesn't want to know where or how Gillen gets his cattle providin' he isn't gonna get into trouble buyin' them from Gillen. Right?"

"Right. So, to avoid trouble, Gillen must change the brands on his stolen cattle to match his own brand or the brand of some other ranch whose cattle he has really bought and is shipping out."

"'Course."

"It takes time to doctor up brands, doesn't it?"

"Yeah; venting brands is work awright."

"Then suppose Gillen's outfit has finished altering the Whitaker brand—"

"And they're tryin' to make time gettin' the shipment to the river?"

"Yes. That might be the reason why they aren't around to stop us."

"Awright. Long as you've answered your own question, what's on your mind now?"

"Just this. If what we've supposed is happening, then our only chance is to overtake Gillen before he reaches the river."

Lute straightened up in his saddle.

"Let's go!" he yelled.

Together they rode southward, into the night, their horses' flashing hoofs pounding a furious beat over the range.

CHAPTER THIRTEEN

THE river gleamed like a silver, satiny ribbon against the backdrop of dark night. There was little sound from the river, just the gentle wash of its water against the half-dozen barges that nestled along the grassy shore. There were no wharfs or docks, no gangplanks, just ramps made of stout planks that led from the shore on to the broad, open surfaces of the barges. There was no one about. The door opened in the tiny cabin on one of the barges, and a woman appeared in the doorway, a slim figure silhouetted against the shaded light of a lamp that was somewhere behind her. A tall, lean man joined her and stood with his arm around her waist. Then they stepped on to the open deck and sauntered forward to the head of the ramp and stopped there and looked northward along the shore line. A man with a lighted lantern swinging from his hand came striding into view. When he came abreast of the couple, he looked at them and stopped a bit hesitantly and debated something with himself; then he trudged up the ramp and stopped again shortly within a step of them.

"According to what you told me, Coady," he said, addressing the tall Texan, "they shoulda been here a couple o' hours ago."

"That's right, McArdle. That's when Gillen said he'd be along."

"Uh-huh. Then how come they haven't showed up yet?"

Coady shrugged. "I wouldn't be knowing. Could be, of course, couldn't it, that somethin' came up that delayed them?"

"Yeah," McArdle admitted. "Could be."

"You know Gillen same's I do," Coady continued. "You know that when he says he's gonna do somethin', he does it, and if he doesn't, there's a blamed good reason for 'im not doin' it."

"Yeah," the man with the lantern said a bit begrudgingly.

"Then keep your shirt on."

"It ain't that I'm doubtin' him, y'understand," McArdle said quickly. "I know he usu'lly keeps his word. It's the time. It's got me worried, I don't mind tellin' you. I'm afraid that if we aren't loaded up and outta here before daylight, we're gonna be plumb outta luck. We'll hafta lay over till t'morrow night."

"Oh, no!" the woman said.

McArdle looked at her obliquely.

"I don't tell the tide what to do or what not to do, lady," he said gruffly. His tone and his manner showed that he resented her.

"Don't you worry now, honey," Coady said to his companion assuringly. His arm tightened around her waist. "Gillen will be along most any minute now, and loadin' his steers aboard these barges won't take any time at all. We'll be outta here half 'n hour after he gets here. You'll see. Look, how's your headache? Ease up any?"

"No," the woman answered, "it's just about the same."

Coady shook his head. "If you'da done like I suggested," he said gently, "and taken that nap, chances are by now it woulda been gone."

"We-ll . . ."

"Why don't you go lay down now? Soon's we get started, I'll let you know, an' you c'n rest easy then. How 'bout it?"

She looked up at him, evidently reconsidering his suggestion; then she smiled. He bent his head and kissed her on the mouth. She smiled again and he released her. He patted her on the backside as she turned away. McArdle and he followed her with their eyes as she retraced her steps to the cabin and went inside. They looked at each other. There was a grin on Coady's face.

"Y'see that, McArdle?" he said. "That's the way to handle a woman. Y'give her a little kiss, a soft word, a pat on the fanny, and you've got her eatin' right outta your hand."

McArdle grunted, obviously unimpressed.

"You might be able to handle some women like that," he said gruffly. "Her kind. But that stuff wouldn't get you anywheres with the other kind, I c'n tell you that."

"Yeah?" Coady retorted. "Women are all alike. Some o' th'm might need a little more coaxin' than others, but way down deep they're all alike. They're all cut outta the same mould."

"Your sayin' so don't make it so," McArdle said, refusing to agree with him. "I've seen that redhead somewheres."

"Could be. She's been places."

"Like where?"

"How do I know where?" Coady demanded. There was annoyance with McArdle in his voice. "All I know is that she's good-lookin' and that she's crazy about me. Do I hafta know anything else about her?"

"Didn't she use to dance in the Oasis?" McArdle asked.

"Yeah, but what's that got to do with it?"

"Nothing," McArdle said calmly. "But I knew I'd seen her before. And now you're takin' her to Texas."

"That's right."

"I dunno whether that's good for Texas or not," McArdle said, "What's she in such a sweat to get away from here for? Got a husband on her trail?"

"Look, McArdle—" Coady began darkly.

"I was just wonderin'," McArdle said. He turned around and started down the ramp. He turned his head and looked up at Coady over his hunched shoulder. "I sure hope Gillen shows up soon."

"You an' me both," Coady answered. He watched McArdle make his way down the ramp. "Ol' buzzard," he muttered to himself. "He's jealous an' he can't keep from showin' it."

He stood at the head of the ramp for another minute or two, his thumbs hooked in his gun belt, then he turned away and sauntered around the deck for a while and finally went into the cabin.

A mile northward, Kirby and Lute Bailey, swinging westward now, pulled their horses to an abrupt, stiff-legged stop when shadowy figures rose up ahead of them. Lute jerked out his gun.

"Hold it a minute," Kirby said quickly. "Don't shoot yet."

A stocky man trudged towards them.

"Awright you two fellers," he called, stopping shortly. "Who are you an' where d'you think you're going?"

Lute peered hard at him, then he turned to speak to Kirby.

"Hey," he said excitedly. "That sounded like Jake Holloway." He pushed past Kirby's detaining hand and rode forward. "Jake, that you?"

"Yep," came the answer. "But who in blazes are you?"

The husky youth laughed. "Lute Bailey, doggone your hide!" he hollered. Kirby rode forward now too and reined in alongside Lute. Other men, with rifles in their hands, came up and gathered around them. "Jake," Lute said, "is Pop around?"

"Nope," Holloway replied. "He an' a hull bunch o' men from town are swingin' along with the Gillen outfit, drivin' it further an' further away from the river all the time."

"Oh," Lute said. "So that's why he didn't come back!"

"He sent us down here to cut off any o' Gillen's polecats," Holloway continued. "Y'know, in case any o' them got away."

"What about the Whitakers?" Lute asked. "They with Pop?"

"Yeah, sure."

"Then Pop knows about Uncle Giff, huh?"

Jake nodded. "The Whitakers told him," he answered. His eyes shifted away from Lute and ranged over Kirby for a moment, then they returned to Lute. "Where are you fellers goin'?"

Lute shifted himself in the saddle.

"Oh, we kinda figgered we'd ride southward a ways," he said casually. "You know, just to have a look around."

Holloway laughed. "You wouldn't wanna fool me, would you?" he demanded.

"What d'you mean, fool you?" Lute asked innocently. "Think we don't know that Coady headed southward, too?"

"He did, hey?"

Holloway's eyes shuttled from Lute to Kirby and back again.

"Y'mean you fellers didn't know that?" he asked.

"Nope," Lute said earnestly.

"Then you do now," Jake said. "He rode into town somewheres 'round early evening, and went into the Oasis. Couple o' minutes later he came out again, and that redheaded dancer they got workin' in there came hustlin' out, too. They went up the street and turned into an alley, and when they came out again both o' th'm were on horses. The last anybody saw o' th'm, they were ridin' southward, an' they were burnin' leather."

"H'm," Lute said, and he glanced at Kirby.

"In case you don't know this either," Holloway went on, "Gillen's flatboats are tied up to shore about a mile south o' here. For my dough, if I was lookin' for that Coady maverick, that's where I'd go lookin'. Your Pop's the boss, and since he don't want any of us to do it, we're stayin' put here. But it's different with you two fellers.

89

There ain't any strings on you, and nobody's tellin' you what to do. Y'know?"

"I know," Lute said with a grin. He straightened up in the saddle. "Be seein' you, Jake. Come on, Kirby. Let's go see if we can't find Mister Coady."

They guided their horses away; when they were free of Holloway's men, they raced off into the night. Lute ranged his horse alongside Kirby's.

"Pop's a good rancher," the youth said. "Knows his business. But he's a helluva lousy sheriff. He'll tell you that himself, so don't think I'm sayin' something I oughtn'ta. He could'a grabbed off Coady and Gillen and got back the Whitaker stock all at one time if he'da come the way we did an' headed for the spot where the boats are tied up. 'Course then we wouldn'ta had the fun we're gonna have gettin' Coady by ourselves."

"From what I've been told about Coady, he's supposed to be a pretty handy man with a gun," Kirby said. "You'd better watch yourself when we get close to him."

"Don't worry about me," Lute retorted, "I c'n take care o' myself."

"Of course," Kirby said.

Lute looked at him oddly; then he swerved his mount away, lashed him with the loose ends of the reins. They pounded over the ground at a furious pace, their horses' hoofs beating a rhythmic drum roll. Five minutes', ten minutes', fifteen minutes' whirlwind riding brought them in sight of the shimmering and silent river. They slowed their panting horses to a trot, and when they spotted the low, shadowy and motionless barges lying so snugly against the shore, they halted and looked about them quickly.

"What d'you think we ought do?" Lute asked in a low tone, inching his mount up against Kirby's.

"Doesn't seem to be anyone around," Kirby remarked, sweeping the barges with his eyes.

"Nope," Lute said. "But there's a lantern or something on the ground in front o' one of the barges. The second, no, the third one. See it? Somebody musta put it there, so the chances are that same somebody is still around. Think we oughta ride down or go in on foot?"

"On our horses," Kirby answered. "In case we have to make a quick getaway."

"Awright."

"If someone appears and challenges us, it might be

wise for us to say we're part of Gillen's outfit. New hands, you know."

"Uh-huh," Lute said. "You all set?"

"All set."

Slowly they rode down the shore line. A voice hailed them, and they pulled up at once, twisted around, trying to locate the man who had called to them. Then they saw him. He came down the ramp from the second barge.

"Hi, partner," Lute called.

"You fellers from Gillen's outfit?" the man asked as he tramped towards them.

"Answer him," Kirby said in a low voice.

"Oh!" Lute said, then he raised his voice a bit, "That's right."

McArdle came up to them. His eyes shuttled from one to the other.

"What's your name?" he asked, looking up at Lute. "And who's your partner?"

Lute eased himself in the saddle.

"I'm Joe Brown," he answered as casually as he could. "My side-kick's name is Smith, Tom Smith."

"Never heard o' either o' you before."

"That ain't surprisin'," Lute said, "Bein' that we only hooked up with Gillen two days ago."

"Oh, I see! I'm McArdle. How many men is Gillen sendin' along to handle the steers he's shippin' out?"

"Dunno for sure," Lute said. "I know we're goin' though. Oh, yeah, McArdle, Gillen told me to see Coady soon's we got here. He around?"

McArdle snorted.

"In the cabin," he said, pointing to it. "But maybe you oughtn't disturb him right now."

"Huh? Why not?"

"Mister Coady's entertainin' his lady love in there," McArdle said, scorn thickening his voice.

Lute laughed. "You don't say? His lady love, hey!"

"Yeah," McArdle said disgustedly. "Some redheaded tramp he picked off a dance-hall floor. He's takin' her back with him to Texas. We c'n stand losin' her up here. I ain't so sure that Texas is gonna be so tickled about 'er though."

Lute grunted and swung himself out of the saddle. He hitched up his pants and shifted his holster mechanically.

"Well, whether Mister Coady likes it or not," he said

91

loudly, "I gotta see him. The boss's orders, y'know, and that's what I go by."

" 'Course," McArdle said.

"Hey, Tom," Lute said, looking up at Kirby. "You keep Mac here company while I go bust up Coady's love-making for a couple o' minutes."

He laughed again, strode off briskly and went plodding up the planked ramp to the deck of the third barge, turned and waved with deceiving calm, marched across the open barge to the cabin door and banged on it loudly.

"Coady!" he called.

Kirby's hand had dropped and tightened around the butt of his gun. He shot a look at McArdle, but the man had turned to watch Lute. Kirby's eyes ranged away, too, to the shadowy figure standing in front of Coady's cabin door. The door opened, and shaded lamplight filled the open doorway for a moment and streamed out over the threshold and on to the deck; then a tall, lean figure was framed in the doorway.

"Yeah?"

"Got somethin' for you, Coady," they heard Lute say.

The youth's voice was clear and strong.

"What is it?" Coady asked, annoyance at being disturbed thickening his voice.

"Here it is," Lute said. They saw his body twist and his right arm jerked. "Reach, you murderin' skunk! Reach!"

There was a breathless moment, an eternally long moment, one that was filled with tenseness and deathly still excitement. Then the imposed silence was rudely and deafeningly shattered. A Colt roared thunderously and defiantly. Hard upon its heels came an answering shot, but it seemed hesitant and puny, and it was lost in the echo of the Colt's blast that seemed to linger in the stilled night air.

They saw Lute sag and totter, and then he stiffened and pitched forward into the cabin. The tall man, evidently side-stepping him, leaped out of the cabin.

"Eva!" he yelled. "Come on!"

He turned and waited and reached into the cabin; there was a cry from within the cabin; then a woman appeared. She came bursting out, and Coady caught her by the hand. Together they ran across the deck towards the ramp. Eva dropped something. She broke away from Coady, wheeled and ran back, caught up whatever it was that she had dropped, wheeled again in almost the same motion and raced back to him and thrust out her hand. He caught it and again they ran towards the ramp. They reached it and skidded to an awkward stop. At the foot of the ramp were two men: one of them was upright, the other was on his hands and knees and now he slumped on the planking and crumpled up limply. The man who stood beside him was curiously like Coady in build and height, and he was looking up at Coady.

It was Eva who spotted the gun in his hand. Perhaps there was something about him that she recognized despite the veiling and distorting night light, something about him that made her recall the scene she had witnessed from the doorway of the Oasis the day that Spanish Joe, in his silk shirt, tailored pants and polished boots, died in the rutted gutter in front of the hotel with a bullet in his vitals. Whatever it was, she screamed and broke away from Coady; he stared at her without understanding, then suddenly backed a bit, twisted and went for his gun.

There was a roar of gunfire; there was a second clap of yellow-flamed thunder, then just as suddenly as it had burst, it ceased, leaving a curious, throbbing echo in the air. Gun smoke swirled about the ramp, lifted and dissolved into nothingness, and everything was normal again. The river washed the grassy shore, and its waters lapped and rolled gently against the caulked sides of the idling barges. Coady lay on the deck, sprawled out on his face, with his gun hand outflung and his gun lying within inches of his lifeless fingers. Eva peered hard at him and screamed again, a piercing scream, and the fading voices of the thundering guns returned and lingered a bit longer; then they died out, but the air was filled with other sounds, the swelling beat of approaching horses and men's voices.

Eva was motionless for a moment, then she gathered her skirts, wheeled around Coady's body and fled down the ramp. She skidded to a faltering stop just as she neared the foot of the ramp. Kirby, his gun still in his hand, looked at her wonderingly, and she stared at him; men rode up and swung themselves off their horses and swarmed forward. She gasped and spun around and raced up the ramp and fled the length of the deck to the cabin and burst into it.

The door swung behind her and latched shut. Men made their way up the ramp to Coady's side. Someone prodded him with a boot toe and, when there was no response, turned him over on his back. Another man stepped on something. He looked down at it. When he saw that it was Coady's gun, he grunted and drew back his right foot and kicked the gun viciously. He caught it squarely and it soared briefly, cleared the edge of the deck and fell into the river with a splash and sank gurglingly.

CHAPTER FOURTEEN

JANE WHITAKER awoke with a start. She thought she had heard hoofbeats and men's voices, although for a moment she wasn't quite certain whether they had been part of a disturbing dream she had had, in which swarms of lawless men had overrun the Whitaker ranch, or if she had really heard them and been awakened by them. She sat up in bed and blinked and quickly threw up her hand to ward off the dazzlingly bright rays of the early morning sun that were streaming into her room. The blind was up, yet she distinctly recalled having drawn it before she prepared herself for bed. It had probably run up on the roller while she was asleep, she decided. She kicked off the covers and swung her legs over the side of the bed. She frowned with annoyance when she couldn't find her slippers. She probed around under the bed with her bare feet until she located them and managed to draw them out, poked her feet into them, got up and went to the window and drew down the blind.

But then—almost at once—she raised one corner of the blind and stole a quick look outside. There were horses in the corral, and leaning over the corral gate and talking quietly among themselves were three men. They were proof, and so were the horses, that she hadn't dreamed she had heard them. One of the men was her father, and the man standing next to him was Uncle John. She couldn't identify the third man; she had to wait until he glanced skyward to get a good look at him, and then she recognized him. It was Gordon Bailey. Her expression indicated that she wasn't particularly pleased to see him. The she spied two other men perched on the top rail of the corral, some fifteen or twenty feet from the others. She recognized Vance Kirby at once; her eyes lingered on him for a moment, then they shuttled away to his companion. She didn't know the man, she told herself. He didn't look familiar to her. He was sitting with his back to the house and, to make recognition just a little more difficult, he was wearing a white, turbanlike bandage wound around his head. But he jumped down suddenly, and when he turned and looked up at Kirby, she saw that it was Lute Bailey. Her wide eyes reflected her surprise. But she turned away from the window and went to her clothes closet.

"I sure wish you'd change your mind about goin' off, Kirby," Lute said.

"I'm afraid I haven't any choice in the matter," Kirby responded.

Lute nodded understandingly. "I know," he said, and then he added sheepishly, "but I can wish, can't I?"

Kirby smiled fleetingly.

"Y'know," Lute went on. "Every time I think o' how you warned me to watch for Coady when we got close to him, an' how I reared up an' told you I could take care o' myself and that you didn't hafta worry about me, I could kick myself."

"Forget it," Kirby said, gesturing.

Lute shook his head. "I was so all-fired smart," he said, "I nearly got my head shot off."

"Forget it, Lute," Kirby said again. "It's past history now."

"Sure," Lute said. "But if it hadn't been for you, I wouldn't be here now. I never saw a man draw like that Coady did. I had him covered an' I was watchin' him awright, and the next thing I knew his gun was exploding right smack in my face. But you got him, beat him to the draw when he went for his gun against you, so that makes you just about the fastest man with a gun that ever——"

"Being that fast hasn't gotten me anywhere," Kirby said with a trace of bitterness in his voice.

"No foolin', Kirby," the youth said eagerly, "y'think it would do you any good if I got Pop to see what he could do?"

Kirby shook his head.

"He can't undo the things I've done, can he?" he asked.

"No," Lute admitted, "he probably can't. But he's pretty smart, Kirby. He might be able to kinda soften those things a little. Y'know? So what d'you say?"

Kirby jumped down.

"Time I got going," he said.

"Y'mean you aren't even gonna wait for breakfast?" Lute asked, his eyes and his voice filled with surprise.

Kirby shook his head. "No," he said. "I'll get something in town."

"Doggone," Lute grumbled. He followed Kirby to the gate.

The conversation between Gordon Bailey and the Whitaker brothers halted at once. The three men looked up as Kirby and Lute rejoined them.

"You fellers must be plumb starved out," Jim Whitaker said. He hitched up his pants. "I'd better go see about breakfast."

"He ain't waitin' for breakfast," Lute said.

"Why not?" Jim asked. He looked at Kirby. "An hour more shouldn't make any difference to you, should it?"

"I think I ought to go now," Kirby said quietly.

"He knows what's best for him to do," Jim Whitaker said. He smiled and shook hands with Kirby. "Good luck, Kirby."

"Thank you."

Kirby gripped hands with Jim, who looked as though he wanted to say something but didn't—or couldn't. He nodded to Gordon Bailey, then he shook hands with Lute who swallowed and hastily turned away.

"If you wanna go up to the house, Son," John said to Kirby, "you go ahead. I'll get your horse for you."

"I would like to."

"'Course," John said. He patted Kirby on the back. "Go 'head."

Kirby smiled his thanks and strode off. The others followed him with their eyes, watched him march around the house, and when he disappeared from sight, they turned away slowly.

"Damn," Lute said, and the others glanced at him and quickly averted their eyes when he looked at them. He shook his head disappointedly and said, "Pop, couldn't you have thought o' something to do or say? Something that would've kept him here with us?"

"There wasn't anything that anyone could have said, Lute, or done," Gordon Bailey said gently.

"To let him go off like that," the youth went on. "All alone, with nobody to turn to an' nothing to look forward to. It just ain't right, specially when we owe him so blamed much. Jim Whitaker wouldn't be here this minute if it hadn't been for Kirby, an' neither would I. But what'd any of us do about it? Not a damned thing."

"Lute," John Whitaker began, "you've gotta look at it this way. Kirby——"

Lute interrupted him with an impatient gesture. "All I know is what I know," he said bitterly and stalked away.

Kirby halted just within reach of the back door. He stood for a moment looking over the yard. There was the spot on which the Whitakers had set up the big easy chair for him so that he might bask in the strengthening sunshine; there Jane had knelt at his feet, giving him his glass of milk or talking with him. He turned away suddenly, forcibly, and went into the house. He stopped again, hat in hand, just inside the doorway. Jane was standing near the kitchen table with her back to the door. Her arms were raised, her hands to her head, tucking in an errant strand of hair.

"Morning, Dad," she said without turning. "Looks like your lazy daughter overslept again. You won't beat me though, will you, if I promise to mend my ways?"

"No, I won't beat you," Kirby said.

She turned quickly and blushed when she saw him standing just beyond her. Quickly she smoothed down the front of her dress; mechanically she ran her hands over her hips. He dropped his hat in one of the chairs that stood against the wall.

"What would you like for breakfast?" she asked.

There was a half-apron slung over a chair, and she caught it up and tied it around her waist. His eyes followed her every move.

"I'm not staying for breakfast," he said when she raised her eyes to his.

Her eyes widened. "Oh!" she said inadequately.

"I'm going."

"Must you go so soon? This morning?"

He smiled at her and came across the room.

"It's a long way to California," he said. He held out his hand to her, and she gave him hers. "Thank you for everything, Jane. You've been very kind to me, and understanding, too."

Her eyes probed his face.

"What's going to become of you?" she asked.

"Oh, I'll be all right," he said lightly.

"Will we hear from you?"

He thought about it for a moment, then he shrugged his shoulders.

"Perhaps," he said. "Perhaps not. I don't really know,

Jane. I've a lifetime to live down and forget. I have to become someone else, so it might be best if I simply went out of everyone's life completely, as though I'd never been in it. Incidentally," he said, and he smiled again, "I know a certain young man who's quite taken with you, young lady. He's a fine young fellow, Jane. I recommend him heartily."

She made no response.

"Lute and I got to know each other pretty well last night," he continued, "and I like him. He's straight-forward and direct, and I like those qualities. You always know where you stand with a person like Lute. You never have to wonder."

"What will you do when you get to California?"

"Oh, I'll find something to keep me busy," he answered. "We were talking about Lute, weren't we?"

"I don't want to talk about him. I want to talk about you."

He was silent for a moment, his head turned the barest bit; her eyes hadn't left his face, and now she studied him as never before. Then his eyes returned to her.

"I had planned to leave here before you were awake," he told her. "Perhaps I should have done that. It would have spared you this."

"I'd never have forgiven you."

"Good-byes are always unpleasant ordeals," he went on as though he hadn't heard her. But she made no attempt to interrupt him, to repeat what she had said. "You plan to say certain things," he mused, "even how you're going to say them, yet when the time comes for your good-bye, you forget everything. It's curious, almost unexplainable, but somehow everything fails you at that particular moment, your memory, your poise—oh, everything; you just stand and look at the person you're bidding good-bye and you're mute and embarrassed. It's only after you've left that the nice things you were going to say return to you in a veritable torrent of words, but then it's too late and you feel utterly miserable. Unfortunately, so does the one you were going to say them to. Funny, isn't it?"

She did not answer. Her eyes clung to him. In turn, his eyes took in every detail of her face and her hair, as though he were committing them to memory. Then he smiled.

"Good-bye, Jane," he said.

"Good-bye, Vance."

Neither of them moved. Then as one they both looked down. He was still holding her hand in his. Their eyes came up together. He smiled, awkwardly this time, and released her hand. He turned suddenly on his heel and went swiftly across the room, caught up his hat and marched out of the house. The door swung shut behind him. Jane was motionless, listening. She heard his boots crunch on the gravel path that led to the barn. When the crunching sound faded, she went slowly out of the kitchen and up the stairs to her room. For a minute she sat on the edge of her bed, staring off into space. Then she stirred and arose with an unusual heaviness, and went to the window.

Gordon Bailey was standing alone, with his back to the corral gate. But there wasn't any sign of her father, or of Uncle John, and she wondered where they had gone. But when her eyes ranged away from the corral, she spied the latter. Lute and he were standing in front of the barn watching Kirby tighten the cinches under his horse's belly. Then he straightened up, climbed up into the saddle. Lute and Uncle John came up to him and he leaned down and shook hands with them. When they stepped back, he wheeled and rode away.

Jane backed to the bed and sank down upon it. Tears filled her eyes and dimmed her vision.

"Jane, honey," a voice said.

She sat up quickly. She hadn't heard the door open. Her father stood for a moment in the doorway, then he came into the room. She wiped her eyes and got to her feet and looked at him. He smiled understandingly and held out his arms to her. She flew across the room. He caught her in his arms and held her tight.

Kirby emerged from Hanley's General Store with his well-filled saddlebags slung over his shoulder. The stage was standing on the opposite side of the street in front of the hotel. He had seen it pull up there some minutes before. He had simply glanced at it then; now he glanced in its direction again as he strode to his horse at the kerb. He stopped suddenly, raised his head.

"Vance."

He turned his head slowly. A woman came towards him. She was a pretty woman, and she was smiling. She was silks and satins and perfumes, and she walked with the easy grace of one born to ballrooms.

"Diane," he said.

"Yes," she breathed. "I've finally found you, Vance, and I'm so glad. Are you—are you glad to see me?"

"It's been a long time," he said. His voice sounded oddly unfamiliar to his ears. "You're—you're looking very well."

"Thank you."

He shifted the saddlebags, easing the weight on his shoulder.

"Why did you follow me here, Diane?" he asked.

"Because I wanted you, Vance. Is it unusual for a woman to want her husband?"

Words, angry ones, torrents of them, surged to his lips, but he checked them and smiled thinly instead.

"And now that you've found me?" he asked.

"I'll never leave you again."

He was himself again, calmer and fully in control of himself. He wouldn't let her know what she had done to him. He would never tell her. Nor would he ask her any questions about herself. That was how it would be.

"I'm on my way to California," he told her. "It's a long way from here. A thousand miles of wild, unsettled and uncivilized country with every possible kind of hazard and peril whichever way you turn. Does that sound inviting to you?"

"The kind of woman I was once, Vance, would have shrunk from such a prospect," she replied calmly. "But I'm not that kind of woman any longer. I'm not afraid."

His mouth tightened. "We'll see," he said grimly. "This won't be a carriage ride, you know. Just horses, as long as they hold out. You'll need rough clothes, and of course, a horse."

"I'll get them."

He wheeled away from her and went to the kerb and slung his saddlebags across his horse's back.

You've got exactly one hour to get what you'll need," he said curtly over his shoulder as he reached for the bridle. "I'll be down the street having something to eat. When you're ready to go, you'll know where to find me."

She smiled again. She had bright-red eager lips and when they parted, he could see her teeth. They were the whitest and the most perfectly formed teeth he had ever seen.

"I'll find you," she said.

He didn't answer. He led his horse away. She watched him for a while, followed him with her eyes, then she gathered her skirts together and swept into Hanley's.

CHAPTER FIFTEEN

It was exactly eleven o'clock, almost four hours to the minute since Kirby had gone. It wasn't quite that long since the Baileys had left, probably an hour less. They had lingered over their breakfast, talking of things in general with the Whitakers, who, when the Baileys finally arose and took their leave, got up from the table, too, and walked with them to the corral. After Gordon and Lute had ridden away, the brothers went off to attend to their own duties around the place.

The stock which Coady and Branch had run off, and which Gillen had bought and included in his downriver shipment, had been recovered in the routing of Gillen's outfit, and now the herd was grazing peacefully in practically the very same spot from which it had been "lifted." Gillen's botched-up venting of the Whitaker "W" brand and his hurried attempts to superimpose another brand without access to the proper irons made necessary a job to which the brothers did not look forward. Both expressed the unhappy opinion that they would probably have to do a completely new branding job before they finished restoring their stock to normalcy, and their eyes glinted when they mentioned Gillen's name. Of course there was one consolation: Gillen would never bother them again, or anyone else for that matter. They had left his bullet-riddled body hunched over in the thick grass of his own spread, and to them that was ample satisfaction.

There were other odd jobs that needed doing, jobs that they had been putting off from day to day, and they admitted somewhat sheepishly, that things had finally caught up with them. They had told Jane not to expect them home for their midday meal; they'd be lucky, Uncle John had grumbled, if they got back by suppertime. So they'd gone off, leaving Jane alone in the house with her own unhappy thoughts to keep her company, and the house was suddenly and strangely hushed because she moved about and worked so quietly.

At eleven o'clock her day's work was finished and be-hind her.

The breakfast dishes had long since been washed and dried and stacked away in their usual places in the cupboard; and the pots and pans, gleaming brightly, a tribute to her industry, hung motionlessly from their individual hooks above the stove. The kitchen floor had been swept, and the chairs—those that stood so rigidly against the walls, and those that stood close to the table —were in their accustomed places. The table scarf and the fancy little crockery piece that graced the vast expanse of table surface, like a tiny island in the middle of a wide lake, were in their usual, orderly places. The upper floor had been taken care of, too. The beds had been made up, the floors swept, the furniture dusted and the rooms aired.

Now there was nothing more to be done. Suppertime was a long way off. The meal would be a comparatively simple one, so she had lots of time in which to prepare it. She stood at the kitchen window and stared out over the grassy span of back-yard lawn. Her eyes sought and found the spot on which the easy chair from the parlor had been set up; there Kirby had sunned himself daily during his convalescence. The lawn was empty now. It was just a piece of ground and a lot of ordinary grass, now that Kirby had gone and the easy chair had been returned to the parlour. She turned away from the window; she stopped abruptly and peered out again. For one fleeting instant she thought she had seen him again, sitting out there in the sun, with his long legs thrust out in front of him and his big hands folded in his lap. Then she realized that it was just her imagination, and she sauntered across the kitchen to the doorway, passed through it to the hall-way and the stairs and went up.

She wandered down the landing. When she came to Kirby's room, she stopped, opened the door and poked her head in. The blind had been raised, and bright sun-shine was streaming into the room. The bed looked strangely unfamiliar without Kirby's long, lean, blanketed figure stretched out on it. She went in on tiptoes and started towards the window to lower the blind, but she stopped suddenly when she realized that the sunlight wouldn't bother him now.

Presently she went downstairs again and wandered aim-lessly through the lower-floor rooms. In the parlour she stopped when she came to the easy chair. She bent over it slightly and ran her hands over the cushions and the arm-rests. There was a warmth to them, a body warmth, as though Kirby had been sitting in it and had just got up. She smiled wistfully and strolled back to the kitchen. For a minute or two she stood at the table, then she went outside.

The sun was warm and it brightened her. She walked along the gravel path, her heels clicking and crunching tiny bits of shale. She glanced in the direction of the barn when she came abreast of it; there was no one in there, and she went on to the corral and leaned over the gate for a while. She wheeled away from it suddenly and strode back to the barn and went inside. She heard Velvet's whinny, and she made her way through the shadows to the mare's stall at the rear and put her arms around her. The mare whinnied again, happily, and after a minute Jane backed her out of the stall, saddled her and climbed up on her back and rode her out of the barn.

Velvet jogged past the tool shed, swung around the corral and, quickening her pace, loped eastward. She was eager to run, but she seemed to sense that Jane was in no mood for it, and she bridled her desire. The range grass was lush and sweet-smelling, and the tiny clusters of wild flowers that dotted it were bright-hued and fragrant. It was a day for living, a day for happiness. But there was no happiness in Jane's heavy heart. A tiny breeze rustled the grass and danced through her hair, but she disregarded it. Stray strands slipped downward over her forehead and over her cheeks, and she simply brushed them away. Some fifteen minutes later they came to the edge of the bank. Jane swung herself out of the saddle. She led Velvet down the slope to the water's edge and left her there to drink while she strolled off a bit. She stopped when she came to a big rock that jutted out over the water and hoisted herself up and sat on it, bent forward, with her feet dangling idly at first, then swinging from side to side. The water was crystal clear. There was a tiny ripple on its smooth surface, and she watched it, held by it. She was startled when she heard a splash. The ripple widened instantly, and she stopped swinging her legs and slowly raised her eyes. Directly across the stream, lying flat on his stomach on a ledgelike rock formation, was Lute Bailey. He extended his right arm to its fullest over the water and dropped a stone into it. There was another splash when the stone struck the water; it plummeted straight down and sank and the ripple widened again.

Lute raised his head. His eyes ranged over the stream. When he spied Jane, he pushed himself backwards off the rocks and got to his feet.

"H'llo, Jane," he called brightly.

"Hello," she answered.

"Awright for me to come over there?" he asked.

She was swinging her legs again. She studied their reflection in the water.

"If you want to," she said.

Velvet looked up. She whinnied, and there was an immediate response from up above on the opposite bank. When Lute whistled there was an answer, a snort, and his horse made his way down the slope. Lute stepped forward to meet him, swung himself up into the saddle and rode across the stream, dismounted and trudged up to the rock on which Jane had perched herself. His horse had stopped beside Velvet. When he nudged the mare with his head, she snorted and backed away from him, trumpeting nasally and indignantly. When he whinnied softly and moved closer to her again she did not rebuff him.

"H'llo," Lute said again, halting in front of Jane and looking up at her.

"Hello."

"Whatcha doin'?"

"Nothing," Jane answered. "Just sitting."

"Oh," he said, and he smiled boyishly. He bent down and picked up a couple of stones. "Sure turned out nice today, didn't it?"

"Very nice."

He tossed a stone into the stream. It struck with a loud splash and when the water shot upward, the two horses backed away from the water's edge in alarm. Lute laughed, and she looked at him wonderingly.

"Water seems to scare horses a heap more'n gunfire does," he explained and flushed a little under her steady gaze.

"Does it?"

"Yeah, sure," he said quickly.

She looked away, across the stream, and he leaned against the rock. When she shifted her position, he looked up at her, but she kept her eyes averted.

"Wonder where he's at now?" Lute asked after a brief silence.

"He?"

"Yeah—Kirby."

"Oh, probably not very far away yet," she answered. "At least, I don't imagine so."

"Come to think of it, he was gonna stop in town an' get himself some breakfast," Lute said. "That must've taken him some time, say about 'n hour. Then he had to get himself some supplies for the trail. You know, bacon an' flour an' stuff. Then he mighta met somebody an' stopped to talk awhile. You know how folks do. Heck, for all we know, he might still be in town, or maybe just headin' out of it. But there's no tellin' of course."

Jane was silent. Lute dug a hole in the soft ground with his boot toe, then he stamped on it, ground his heel into the spot and levelled it off again.

"He's awright, Kirby is," he said shortly. "I like him."

Jane drew up her legs. She tucked her knees under her chin.

"Y'know," Lute began again, "when a feller's got so much to offer, looks an' education an' the rest, like Kirby has, and then can't find anything to do with what he's got, it's sure tough on him. What d'you suppose is gonna be the end of him? Where d'you suppose he's gonna wind up?"

"He—he'll be all right," she said without looking up.

"Y' think so? I don't."

He looked at her, waiting for her to say something; when she made no reply, he straightened up and moved away from the rock to the very edge of the water, poked at a half-buried stone with his boot toe, finally forced it loose from the dirt and pushed it into the stream. It sank with a gentle murmur, and a tiny ripple appeared above it.

"I sure hope everything works out for him," he said over his shoulder. "He's all by himself. It's different with us. We've got folks, our fathers, that is, an' our homes. He hasn't got a damned—oh, excuse me, Jane—he hasn't got anything or anybody. Gee, it must be doggoned tough when a feller like him gets sick or gets into trouble. What's he do then? Who's he turn to?"

"Lute, please!"

He turned around to her. "S'matter?" he asked.

She climbed down from the rock, wheeled and went quickly to Velvet's side.

"I've got to go now," she said.

He came around the rock.

"Want me to ride back with you?" he asked hopefully, looking at her closely.

She shook her head, reaching at the same time for the reins.

"No," she said. "I—I'd rather you didn't."

"Awright, Janey," he said. There was disappointment in his voice. "You gonna come down here again later on, or maybe tomorrow?"

"I don't know. I don't think so."

"How would it be if I kinda rode by your place some time this evening?" he asked eagerly. "Would it be aw-right? 'Less, of course, you've got something you've gotta do."

"N-o," she said slowly. Then she looked up at him and gave him a quick smile. "I won't have anything to do this evening."

"Swell," he said, beaming. "I'll be around!"

He watched her lead Velvet up the bank to the top, saw her mount and wheel the mare.

"G'bye for now!" he yelled.

There was no answer, nothing but the swift beat of Velvet's hoofs; it faded out almost at once due to the cush-ioning grass. Lute was motionless for a minute, then he went to his horse, vaulted up into the saddle and wheeled in practically the same movement and rode across the stream to the Bailey side.

Jane was surprised, when she entered the house, to find that her father and uncle had returned. The latter was setting the table; he looked up as she came into the kitchen and grinned. Her father was frying something at the stove. She flew across the room to his side.

"Oh, I'll do that, Dad!" she said quickly. "I didn't ex-pect you back so soon or I wouldn't have gone off. Uncle John said you'd be lucky if you got back by nightfall."

Jim Whitaker smiled at her and yielded the frying pan without protest, turned and sauntered over to his chair and seated himself in it.

"Wasn't as much of a job as we figgered it would be," he told her.

"Anyway, what we did this morning'll more'n do for now," Uncle John added. He rubbed his nose with the back of his hand and eyed the table. "Let's see now. Salt, pepper, sugar, butter, bread. Guess I didn't forget any-thing."

He swung his chair away from the table and straddled

it. Jane served their dinner shortly, and John swung his chair around. The brothers talked throughout the meal, maintaining a light, brisk conversation that was designed to draw Jane's thoughts away from herself, and every now and then one of them would address his remarks to her in an effort to get her to comment or answer. But Jane had nothing to say. She ate with little appetite, toying with her food rather than eating it. Uncle John, who was watching her, suddenly leaned over the table.

"Here, here, young un," he said severely, shaking a thick, warning finger at her. "You c'n do better than that. We like our womenfolk to be pretty awright, but we like 'em with some meat on their bones. Now you get to work on what's on your plate or I'll take off my belt to you. Stay where you are, Jim. I'll pour the coffee."

Jim Whitaker had been watching his daughter, too, but wisely he had refrained from making any comment. What he had to say to her, he would say when they were alone. Usually, when dinner was over, he would get up, pick up his hat and saunter to the door, open it, and then, standing in the doorway he would look at John who would frown, mumble something to himself and slowly get up from his chair and follow him out. This time Jim took out his pipe, struck a match to it, and sat back. John kept looking at his brother, trying vainly to catch his eye. Finally, frowning, he pushed back from the table and got to his feet. Just then Jim looked up at him, nodded and jerked his head in the direction of the door. John smiled fleetingly and picked up his hat.

"I'm done sittin' around after I've eaten," he announced. "Makes a feller fat an' lazy. Y'know somethin', Jim? I kinda feel like I've put on some weight lately. What d'you think?"

"Oh, I dunno," Jim replied, eyeing him. "I wouldn't worry about it though. You c'n stand another ten pounds."

"Huh," John snorted. "Ten pounds, hey? I'm bustin' out o' my clothes the way it is. What d'you want me to do? Put on some more weight an' go 'round wearing a blanket instead o' my pants?"

He pinched Jane's cheek, and she looked up at him and smiled. He stalked out of the house. Jane arose and started to clear away the dishes, but her father reached out, took her by the hand and brought her close to him.

"Used to be a time when you seemed to like sittin' on my lap," he remarked.

She needed no urging; she perched herself on his knees and pillowed her head on his shoulder. When his arms tightened around her, she buried her face in his neck. He patted her gently on the back.

"All right, Janey," he said. "Let's face it now. What c'n we do?"

It was half an hour later when Jim Whitaker came plodding down the path from the house. He looked towards the corral for a sign of John, then when he came abreast of the door of the barn, he stopped and peered inside.

"P-sst!"

Jim jerked his head towards a far corner. It was shadowy there, and he couldn't see anything. Then there was a movement, a step, and a hand reached out and touched him.

"In here, Jim," he heard John say in a low voice. "Don't want her to see us talkin'."

Jim stepped into the barn, and his brother guided him away from the door.

"Awright," John said briskly. "Let's have it. How is she now?"

Jim shrugged his shoulders and his brother frowned.

"What's that supposed to mean?" he demanded.

"It's supposed to mean that I don't know 'nymore now than I did before," Jim retorted.

"That's fine. What are we gonna do?"

Jim shook his head. "Damned if I know," he replied.

"If only Kirby didn't have a wife," John said. "Then it would be a cinch."

"I know."

"I'd tell Janey to go after him," John continued. "If she couldn't bring him back here, then I'd tell her to go anywheres she could with him, California, Mexico, Canada, anywhere."

"Uh-huh," Jim said wearily. "But bein' that he's got a wife already—"

"That's what licks us."

"Right. F'r my dough, the best thing she can do now is forget him."

John looked at him obliquely.

"Yeah, sure," he said scornfully. "That's a heap easier said than done. You oughta know better'n to say anything as dumb as that."

"I don't know what else she can do," Jim said doggedly.

He looked hard at his brother. "Wait a minute. You sound like you might have an idea or somethin'."

"Nope," John said sadly, shaking his head. "I haven't. All I can do is hope that somethin' happens that'll fix things up for that young un."

Jim Whitaker grunted.

"Well, while you're busy hopin', I'll go tend to what needs doin' around here. See you later."

CHAPTER SIXTEEN

IT was about half past eight, and the darkness had already begun to deepen and settle. In the light of the lamp on the kitchen table, with his account books opened in front of him and a stub of a pencil gripped tightly in his hand, Jim Whitaker was working over a column of figures. Three times he had added the column, and three times he had come up with a different total. He slammed the stub down on the table and sat back frowning. Opposite him, his brother John was dozing in a chair, his head bowed and his chin resting on his chest and his hands folded in his lap. When his deep breathing became laboured and he snored, Jim glared at him for a minute and finally leaned over the table and poked him in the shoulder.

"Doggone it, John," he spluttered. "If you're so blamed all in, why in thunder don't you go to bed, huh?"

John's head jerked up.

"Who says I'm all in?" he demanded. He blinked in the glare of the lamplight. "Y'got that danged thing turned up so high, you'd think you were tryin' to outshine the moon."

Jim grunted and turned the light down a bit. John rubbed his nose with the back of his hand.

"It's gettin' so around here lately," he grumbled, "a feller can't close his eyes to rest them without somebody hoppin' all over him an' chasin' him off to bed."

"In case you don't know it," Jim retorted stiffly, "you were snorin' away like all get-out. How d'you expect me to add up this stuff with all that racket goin' on, huh?"

John Whitaker scoffed, gesturing expansively to indicate his scorn.

"I never snore an' you know it, doggone it," he said gruffly. "The trouble with you is, you can't add. What's more, you know it, only you won't own up to it. So you blame it on me."

There was a sudden clatter of hoofs; they looked at each other.

"Sounds like somebody's comin'," John said presently as the hoofbeats swelled.

"Wouldn't be surprised," Jim said dryly.

He closed his ledgers and put the pencil in his pocket. Then they heard footsteps outside, and finally there was a sharp knock on the door.

"H'm," Jim mused. "Wonder who it is this time o' night?"

"There's one sure way to find out," his brother said curtly. "That's by openin' the door."

"You think that up all by yourself?" Jim asked.

He frowned again, arose and hitched up his pants, strode to the door and opened it.

"Evenin', Mr. Whitaker," John heard a boyish voice say. He turned around in his chair. Lute Bailey, hat in hand, stood in the doorway.

"Oh, h'llo, Lute," Jim answered. He backed a bit, opening the door wider. "Come in."

"I was ridin' past," Lute explained somewhat lamely and he flushed, "an' I got the idea I oughta stop an' see how Janey was doin'."

"Uh-huh," Jim said. "Come in, boy. Come in."

Lute stepped inside. The door closed behind him.

"Oh, good evenin', Mr. Whitaker," he said to John.

"Evenin', Lute," John answered. He climbed to his feet stiffly, yawned and stretched himself, grinned at Lute and rubbed his nose, hitched up his pants and sauntered out to the foot of the stairs. "Janey!"

"Yes?"

"Some young feller's here to see you," Uncle John said. He turned his head and winked at Lute. "Got himself all shined up. Hair slicked down, face scrubbed. Even got 'imself a crease in his pants . . . What'd you say, Janey? . . . Who is he? Wait'll I ask him."

Lute grinned sheepishly. He shifted his weight from one leg to the other and ran his finger around the sweatband of his hat.

"Janey!" John called. "He says his name's Bailey, Lute Bailey. He tells me you know him. That right?"

"Oh, Uncle John!"

He laughed softly, deep down in his throat, and turned

110

away from the stairs and retraced his steps to the kitchen. He patted Lute on the back lightly as he passed him.

"Sit down, Son," he said, nodding towards a chair that stood against the wall behind the husky youth.

"Oh, that's awright, Mr. Whitaker!" Lute said quickly. I don't mind standin'."

"I do, so I'll sit," John said over his shoulder as he went back to his chair. He seated himself and yawned again and shook his head. Jim who had returned to his chair looked at him oddly, and John said, "Can't understand it. Must've been somethin' I had for supper that's made me so blamed sleepy."

"You didn't have anything different than I had," Jim retorted.

There was a quick, light step on the stairs, then Jane came into the room. She was carrying her coat over her arm. She gave Lute a smile.

"Hello, Lute," she said.

"Evenin', Jane," he responded, and he reddened a bit.

She handed him her coat and he looked at it blankly; but when she simply turned her back to him, he understood what was expected of him. He crumpled his hat and shoved it under his arm in order to free both of his hands and held her coat open for her. She pushed her arms into the sleeves.

"Thank you," she said. She buttoned the coat about her and turned to him. "Shall we walk a little, Lute?"

"It's awright with me," he answered.

Jane moved around the table to her father's side, bent over him and brushed his cheeks with her lips.

"Kinda dark outside," John said as she moved towards him. "Want me to go hang some lanterns around so's you c'n see where you're goin'?"

She didn't answer. She came up behind him and rumpled his hair and stepped past him quickly, avoiding the hand he put out. Lute, grinning, followed her to the door. He stepped ahead of her suddenly, opened the door and held it wide. He flashed a smile behind him at John Whitaker and followed Jane out of the house. Lute's horse whinnied when they came abreast of him; when they passed him he pawed the ground and whinnied again, shrilly, this time, as though he were trying to remind them that they had forgotten him. They strolled down the path. The barn just ahead of them and the tool shed a little beyond the barn were dark and shadowy, distorted in size and structure by the night light. They cut away diagonally towards the corral. The worn top bars shone against the dark background. They halted when they came to the gate and leaned over it. There was a slight chill in the air and a tiny breeze came up and whipped the trampled dust about for a moment or two, just long enough to make Jane turn up her coat collar and Lute put on his hat. Then the breeze died down. Lute looked skyward.

"Swell moon tonight," he said.

Jane raised her eyes skyward, too.

"Yes," she said. "Isn't it?"

He turned to her suddenly.

"You're prettier'n any girl I ever knew," he said. "You know that?"

"Thank you, Lute," she said graciously.

"Yeah, an' a million times nicer, too," he blurted out.

She turned her head and looked at him and, evidently embarrassed by his outburst and her eyes, he looked away. But presently, when he was himself again, aided no doubt by the cloaking and covering darkness, he folded his arms on the top rail and rested his chin on them. It gave Jane an opportunity to steal a sidelong, appraising look at him. He was big, but he was still such a boy. Unconsciously she was comparing him with Kirby. It wasn't fair to Lute to compare them, she admitted. He was a boy and Kirby was a man. Yet she knew Lute would never be a Kirby. It wasn't in him. He might be a big man when he matured, not simply in a physical sense but in other ways, too; but he would still suffer by comparison with Kirby.

"You're awf'lly quiet," Lute said after a while. "What are you thinkin' about?"

"Oh-h . . . things."

She waited for his next question; she knew what it would be and she was prepared for it.

"About Kirby?"

"About him, too."

"Wish you'd think about me some time," he said.

He tried to say it lightly, and he failed; she pretended not to notice it.

"I do think about you," she said.

His head jerked around.

"Y'do?" he asked. "On the level?"

"On the level, Lute."

"I think about you all the time," he went on, looking

away again. "I see your face everywhere I turn, everywhere I go. It's been that way right from the beginning, I guess, right from the first time I saw you, Jane . . ."

"Yes?"

"Jane, I've always been crazy about you," he said with tragic earnestness. Then as though to cover his embarrassment, he added hastily, "Half the ranch is mine now. Pop's made me an even partner. What d'you think o' that?"

"Lute, I think it's wonderful!"

"Yeah, I do, too." He straightened up and turned to her, resting his right arm on the top rail. There was a smile on his face, a happy, eager smile, and his voice reflected the excitement within him. "We're really gonna make somethin' out've the old place. We've been talkin' about what we're gonna do, an' Pop's just as excited about it as I am. Who knows, but maybe some day it'll be the biggest an' the richest spread in the hull—the whole county. Now that'd be something, wouldn't it, Jane?"

"It would indeed, Lute."

"Yeah," he said. But then he averted his eyes as he rested both arms on the gate. "But a man can't be expected to do big things by himself. It isn't meant to be. He's gotta have help. Oh, I don't mean somebody to ride fence for 'im, or help with the other work around the place. He's got to have somebody who knows him an' understands him an' knows what he's aimin' for. Somebody who—who loves him."

"Oh," she said.

"You can hire all the hands you want," he continued. "So that ain't it. What I mean is—we-ll—you know what I mean, Jane. Don't you?"

"You mean a wife, Lute."

"Uh-huh," he said, and he seemed relieved. "Then everything would be just right. Y'know somethin' else, Jane? I'll bet you can't name many fellers anywheres near my age around these parts who are partners in a good-payin' spread. That's somethin' to think about. Y'know? An' wait till we go into town t'morrow an' sign the papers. Pop wants it made legal. Bet there'll be lots o' girls who'll be interested in me when word gets around that I'm half owner of our place. But they don't hafta bother. I don't want any part o' th'm. None o' th'm."

He paused, evidently waiting for her to say something; it was as though he had given her her cue, and it was now her turn to express herself. When she remained silent, she knew she had disappointed him, perhaps failed him. She was certain of it almost at once, when he spoke again.

"No," he said again with a curious heaviness in his voice. "They aren't for me. They aren't the kind I want." He turned his head and looked back towards the house for a moment, then he swung around again. "I want you, Jane. Nobody else. I'd be awf'lly good to you. Honest, I would. I'd do everything I could to make you happy."

"Lute—"

He stopped her with a gesture.

"You don't hafta say anything yet, Janey," he said quickly. "If you'll just think about it for a while. Awright?"

There was a crunching sound, heavy, booted steps on the gravel path, and they turned together. Someone who was shadowy and unrecognizable in the night light came towards them from the direction of the house.

"H'llo," a voice called. It was John Whitaker. He came up to them. "I was wonderin' what kind of a night it was." Jane moved closer to him. She slipped her arm through his, and he looked at her and patted her hand. "Hate to bother you tonight, Jane, but I was kinda figgerin' on wearin' that old leather jacket o' mine tomorrow. I hauled it out've the closet an' looked it over, an' I'm doggoned if every last button on it ain't busted. Think you might be able to do somethin' about it before you turn in, providin' of course that it ain't too late by then?"

"Of course, Uncle John."

"I think I oughta be goin'," Lute said. "Must be after nine by now."

"It was twenty after when I came out," John said.

"Gee," Lute said. "It's later'n I figgured it was. And I've got a dozen things to do before I can turn in. Jane, you walkin' around to the back door? I left my horse tied up there, you know."

"Janey," Uncle John said, "why don't you and Lute—"

"No," Jane said firmly, interrupting him. "You're going in too. This is no time for you to go wandering about. Come on. You're coming with us."

Uncle John laughed.

"Y'see that, Lute?" he said to the youth. "That's what happens to you when there's a woman in your life. You get bossed around from morning to night an' without a letup f'r meals. It's somethin' awful, believe me. And this

114

young un, well, she's just about the bossiest critter I ever laid eyes on. She's always crackin' the whip."

"I'll bet," Lute said with a light laugh.

John shrugged his shoulders.

"You don't hafta take my word for it, y'know," he said. "Go lookit her father. Poor feller, he's just about done in from bein' hounded."

"All right, Uncle John," Jane said severely. "That will do. Incidentally, where did I leave my whip?"

John grinned. "Doggoned if I'm gonna tell you," he answered. "Come on. We'll give Lute a send-off."

They trooped around the house to the rear. The back door opened, and Jim Whitaker appeared in the doorway.

"There y'are, Lute," John said, gesturing in his brother's direction. "Got the whole blamed family on hand to see you off. Can't ask for anything more, can you?"

"No, guess not," Lute answered.

He stepped up to his horse, untied him and climbed up astride him.

"It's dark, young feller, so you'd better watch yourself goin' home," Jim called from the doorway. Lute wheeled his mount. "You takin' a short cut?"

"Yeah, sure," the youth replied, settling himself in the saddle. "Through the stream. Saves me more'n a mile of ridin' goin' that way."

"Yeah, but watch yourself," Jim repeated.

"G'night!" Lute flung at them as he spurred his horse and loped away.

"G'night!" the Whitakers answered.

There was a brief flurry of hoofbeats, but then they began to fade out, and shortly after they were gone altogether. Jim backed a bit, holding the door wide; after Jane and John were inside, he closed and bolted the door and went back to his account books. Jane took off her coat and folded it over the back of a chair.

"Where's the jacket, Uncle John?" she asked.

"Huh? The jacket? Oh, it's upstairs."

"Come on," she commanded. "We'll have a look at it. It seems to me, though, that I changed all the buttons on your jacket and on Dad's just a couple of weeks ago. Now I can't understand how all your buttons should suddenly—"

"I don't go 'round bustin' them, I'll have you know, doggone it!" John sputtered with a show of indignation.

She put her hands on his shoulders and turned him

around and herded him out of the room and up the stairs. In his room she went directly to his closet, opened it and took out the leather jacket.

"Turn up the lamp, please," she said. The light flamed brightly. "Uncle John!"

"Huh?"

"Why, there isn't a single broken button on——"

He took the jacket out of her hands and slung it on the bed. He looked at her and smiled.

"I know," he said. "I kinda got the idea that maybe you had had enough o' Lute for one day, so I——"

"You're an old fraud," she said, interrupting him. She bent towards him and kissed him on the cheek. "But you're a precious one. How about some coffee before we turn in?"

"I'm your man!"

"Come on then!" she said as she turned towards the door. "Let's see what we can find to go with the coffee!"

The dawn breeze droned through the grass, and the three horses that were tied up close to the brush stirred and pawed the ground and milled about for a moment. Despite the fact that they subsided when the wind swerved and raced away, the sound of their moving about was enough to awake Kirby; he sat up, looked over in their direction, pushed off his blanket and climbed to his feet. He yawned and stretched himself; he stopped abruptly and made a wry face. There was a stiffness in his legs and a soreness in his shoulder. He rubbed himself and stamped about on the ground in an effort to stimulate blood circulation in his legs, and after a while he felt better.

He glanced at the blanket-covered figure asleep in the grass a dozen feet beyond him. Yesterday had been a long day; they'd had an even longer ride, and while it had been hard on him, he admitted that it must have been doubly hard on her. But she hadn't complained. Of course it was only the first day; there'd be lots of other days, hundreds of them before they reached California, and perhaps long before they got there, she'd change.

His saddlebags were heaped on the ground between them. A small, sturdy trunk that she had purchased for her own use stood somewhat apart from the saddlebags, closer to her than to him. Her clothes were in the trunk, the rich, satiny dress she had worn when they met in town, the plumed and ribboned hat, and the rest of her finery.

Doubtless she had had some sort of bag for her things on the stage; he hadn't seen any, but he assumed she had had one somewhere, probably at the hotel in Jake Holloway's keeping, to be called for when she was ready to take the outbound stage. She had probably disposed of it, perhaps in trade or part payment for the trunk. He had just emerged from the restaurant when she appeared clad in dungarees, boots, sweater and jacket, leading two horses that she had bought, one to ride, the other to serve as a carrier. The trunk was lashed to the second animal's back; he had glanced at it disinterestedly and he had made no comment. If she wanted a pack horse, he had told himself, it was all right with him. It didn't matter very much one way or another. Neither did she.

They had made their first stop at noontime. She hadn't asked him to do it; he had done it of his own accord. He produced the coffeepot, the coffee and the water, and he went about preparing the coffee just as he would have done if he had been alone. He had bought a bag of biscuits in the restaurant in town; the biscuits, warmed up, and the coffee formed their dinner. They had halted for the night just after sundown. Night came on swiftly on the open range, and there would have been nothing gained by pushing on in the gathering and deepening darkness. Again it was he who provided the food and prepared their meal, a panful of crisp, crackling bacon, some more of the biscuits, warmed up as before, and some fresh coffee.

They hadn't talked much during the day; they had talked a bit during and after their supper, a polite conversation that had nothing of a personal nature in it, but the conversation was forced and the lapses of silence that punctuated the snatches of talk were awkward, and after a while they simply sat back. When Diane began to twist and fidget, he decided she was overtired; he arose and unslung her bedroll and blankets and opened them for her; then he moved away and laid out his own blankets. There was a simple "Good night," and that was all. It was fantastic and incredible, but it was true nevertheless.

Now she lay a dozen feet away, rolled up in her blankets, asleep on her side with her back to him. He looked at her and shook his head. He had never expected to see her again, yet there she was.

He had had a difficult time of it with Jane, not with her personally, but with his disturbing thoughts of her. A dozen times that morning on his way to town he had stopped his horse, wheeled him around and started back to the Whitaker place. But each time he had managed to check himself and go on his way again. It hadn't been easy, but he told himself he was glad he had withstood the temptation. Now he was probably fifty miles from the Whitaker place. By tomorrow night it would be a hundred miles, and every night after that the distance between them would be increasingly greater.

He was in love with Jane. He acknowledged it; of course he hadn't admitted it to her despite the fact that he knew she was aware of it. He hadn't had the right to tell her. He hadn't wanted to hurt her, but he had; in that last moment of parting, when he had held her hand in his, he had read it in her eyes. She was in love with him. He shook his head sadly. He hadn't wanted that to happen. It didn't matter that he had been hurt; that fact that she had been hurt mattered greatly. He'd have given anything to have saved her from that. But now it was too late. The damage had been done.

There was only one thing he could do for her. He had told her he was going out of her life for ever. He would keep that promise. She would never hear anything from him. Ridding herself of thoughts of him would be strictly up to her. He wouldn't be able to help her on that score. She would have to do it alone. Oh, it wouldn't be easy for her, particularly at first. But pain was part of forgetting, and she would have to suffer before she could forget.

The dawn sky was still drab and empty. He went back to his blankets and rolled up in them and burrowed deep in their warm folds. He closed his eyes. Jane's face promptly appeared and, even though he struggled to put her out of his thoughts, her vision persisted. He knew then he would never be able to forget her. He knew too that he would always want her. And when he finally dozed off again, the dream that tormented him revolved around Jane.

CHAPTER SEVENTEEN

THE long days that followed witnessed a curious transformation in the Whitakers. It was probably more of a deterioration than a change. It came about first in Jane; then it seemed to communicate itself to her father and her uncle, and finally, to the house in which they lived.

Taking them in that order, Jane took to moving about the house in a strangely tight-lipped and silent way, performing her duties as usual, but everything she did, from cooking to cleaning, was done more or less mechanically; as time went on, her work became laboured and listless. Breakfast for the three Whitakers became a thing of the past, because Jane seldom appeared before the middle of the morning, long after Jim and John Whitaker had left the house. Dinner took the form of sandwiches, which the men prepared for themselves and which they ate while at work; supper became a silent, tasteless and thoroughly unattractive session. Jane spent more and more time in the seclusion of her room, at first, with the door closed, and later, with it locked. She ate with a decreasing appetite; her father and uncle watched her, helplessly and inadequately, and soon her silence began to take effect on them too.

In the evening, after the supper dishes had been done and the kitchen had been put to rights, Jane would go upstairs. The two men would sit as usual at the kitchen table with the lamp between them, casting off a perfect circle of light that stopped at the edge of the table and left the rest of the room steeped in shadows. John didn't nap as he used to, and Jim didn't seem to have the heart or the interest for his account books. There was little conversation, for neither seemed to have much to say. Even the usual nightly cup of coffee before they trudged upstairs to bed had been done away with. Nothing was the same with the Whitakers. Everything had changed.

Then the house began to show the effect of the transformation. It was a silent house now, filled with the tiny, throbbing echoes of voices and footsteps rather than actual sound.

Lute Bailey came to the house regularly. But Jane would not see him. He listened without comment to John's lamely offered excuses, accepting the faltering explanations that Jane had a bad headache, that she was tired, or that she wasn't feeling very well. John always escorted Lute to the door and always gave him a friendly pat on the back, and always, after the youth had gone, he would shake his head sadly as he closed the door. Lute haunted the stream, but it was wasted effort, since Jane showed no desire to ride. Then in a desperate effort to see her, he took to riding up to the house during the early afternoon hours; at first he did not go all the way up to the door, halting at a distance of some thirty or forty feet and waiting there, hoping that she would have occasion to come outside and that he could get a glimpse of her. Then after a few days of futile hope, he rode up to the door and knocked on it. There was no answer. He waited a few minutes, and then he repeated the knock. Presently Jim Whitaker appeared in the doorway.

"Oh, h'llo, Lute," he said.

"H'llo, Mr. Whitaker," Lute said.

"Come in, Boy," Jim said, holding the door wide. Lute stepped inside. He looked around the room quickly. He flushed when he found Jim watching him. "Sit down, Lute."

He took the youth's hat from him and dropped it in a chair near the door, followed him across the room to the table where he spun a chair around for him. Then he seated himself, too, and looked up. The house was so quiet. Lute's eyes ranged past Jim to the stairway.

"She isn't here, Son," Jim said gently and Lute looked at him and sat back in his chair.

"Oh," he said. "She go to town?"

"No," Jim answered with a heaviness that made Lute start. "She's gone farther than that. She's gone after Kirby."

The youth's eyes were wide with surprise. "Gone after him? Y'mean she went off by herself?"

"No. With her Uncle John."

There was a moment's silence.

"How'll she know where to look for him?" Lute asked shortly.

"She has a pretty good idea of where he's gone," Jim replied. "California."

"Yeah, I know," Lute said. "Leastways, that's where he said he was goin'. But, heck, that's a long ways from here. Maybe a thousand miles."

"More or less."

"An' there ain't just one way o' getting there either," Lute hastened to point out. "She might spend a year tryin' to find him, an' never come anywheres near him."

"I know that, Son," Jim said, heavily again.

Lute looked bewildered. He shook his head.

"You shouldn'ta let her go, Mr. Whitaker," he said presently. "That was a mistake. It's bad country. An' just the two o' them against anything that might come up. Gee." He got up slowly. "What happens if she don't find him?"

he asked. "She gonna spend the rest of 'er life chasin' around for him?"

"She'll come back."

"Oh."

"Uncle John went along with her just to make sure she finds Kirby. Of course, if she doesn't find him, Uncle John will bring her back."

"Uh-huh. But supposin' she does find Kirby? What happens then? What about his wife?"

"I don't know the answer to that, Lute."

"He can't marry Jane while he's still married to the other one, can he?" the husky youth demanded.

" 'Course not."

"Then why in thunder did she go after him?"

"Lute—"

"It just don't make sense to me," Lute went on. "I'm doggoned if it does."

Jim Whitaker held his tongue. There was no point in arguing. Lute pushed his chair close in to the table. He suddenly jerked his head up.

"When did they go?" he asked.

"Yesterday morning."

"Uh-huh," Lute said thoughtfully. He wheeled and strode across the room, caught up his hat, opened the door and looked back over his shoulder. " 'Bye!"

" 'Bye, Lute," Jim answered.

He arose as Lute went out, went quickly to the swinging door and caught it before it could slam. He stood in the doorway for a moment, watched Lute climb up on his horse, saw him wheel and lash his mount and send him pounding away. The clatter of hoofs echoed briefly. When it faded out, Jim closed the door and trudged back to his chair and sat down again. But after a while he got to his feet and wandered aimlessly around the house. He went out presently and walked down the gravel path to the barn. He poked his head inside. He heard the swish of a horse's tail against the wooden sides of a stall, and he sauntered off again, down to the corral. He halted there and leaned over the gate for a minute or two, then he perched himself on the top rail and stared moodily over the fields beyond the corral. A little later he climbed down and marched back to the barn and tramped inside and disappeared in the shadowy rear. Minutes later there was a clatter of hoofs on the barn's wooden floor, and Jim rode out astride his horse.

He loped past the corral and headed eastward. His horse was eager to run, and he bounded away, lengthening his stride and quickening his pace until Jim, who was in no particular hurry, checked him, disregarding the animal's protesting snorts and his struggles for his head, and slowed him to a canter. The house, the barn, the corral, everything fell away behind them as they rode over the range. Some fifteen minutes later they came in sight of the Whitaker stock grazing unconcernedly along the easterly fence, the dividing line between the Whitaker and Bailey ranches. Jim rode closer, pulled up shortly, eased himself in the saddle and looked around. A bit southward, less than a quarter of a mile away, but also against the fence, although on their own side of it, were the Bailey steers. He rode slowly along the fence, following it from one end to the other and then on to the bank over the stream where he idled again for a while. When idleness began to irk him, he wheeled his mount away and rode home.

It was a long time since Jim had had to prepare his own meals. Jane had left him some cold meat for the previous night, but that was gone. Now he set about readying his supper in rather awkward fashion. But finally it was done, and he set a place for himself at the table. Every time he sat down he realized that he had forgotten something else, first the salt, then the butter, the sugar and finally a knife, and frowning, he had to get up again.

"Damnation," he muttered. "This is enough to drive a man to drink."

But finally, he had everything he needed, and he was able to proceed with his eating. The remains of an apple pie that Jane had baked a couple of days before, and two cups of coffee topped off the meal and, when he sat back, he was thoroughly satisfied. He shifted himself into a more comfortable position, took out his pipe and lit it. Then he heard the beat of approaching hoofs, and he looked annoyed again.

"Lute," he muttered to himself.

He got to his feet and set about clearing the table. He was about half-way through the process of transferring his supper dishes from the table to the sink when there was a rap on the door.

"Damn," he grumbled. Then he yelled, "It's open. Come on in, Lute!"

The door opened and a short, stocky figure filled the doorway.

"Evening, Jim."

Jim turned his head.

"Well, for Pete's sake!" he said. "Jake Holloway!"

The stage-line owner grinned at him.

"In the flesh," he said wryly. "And I seem to be gettin' more of it all the time."

Jim came forward, patted Jake on the back and kicked the door shut.

"What are you doin' out this way?" he asked. "Kinda off the trail for you, isn't it?"

"Well, you haven't been in town lately," Holloway said. "So I kinda figgered I'd ride out here an' see how you were doin' all by yourself."

Jim hitched up his pants.

"This business of livin' alone and likin' it is a lot o' hogwash, an' don't let anybody tell you different," he declared. "I don't like it one little bit, an' I don't mind sayin' so right out loud. It's lousy. But wait a minute now. That remark o' yours nearly got by me. How'd you know I was all alone?"

"How d'you think?" Jake retorted. "Don't you know I've got a flock o' vultures flyin' around, an' they keep me posted on everything that goes on?"

"Oh, you musta seen John and Jane."

" 'Course!"

"Sit down, Jake."

Holloway tossed his hat aside. He plodded forward to the table, took the chair that Jim had been sitting in, moved it farther out from the table, seated himself and looked up. Jim sat down on the opposite side of the table, pushed some of the dishes aside and made room for his folded arms.

"So you know Jane an' John've gone," he mused.

"That's why I was hopin' I'd see you," Holloway told him. He leaned over the table. "Jim, that Kirby's wife was in town. She went westward with him."

Jim's jaws closed tight. Jake's thick fingers drummed on the surface of the table.

"Fine-lookin' woman, awright," he continued. "Don't think I ever saw a prettier one. She came in on the stage. As a matter o' fact, she'd just gotten off it when Kirby came outta Hanley's place, and she went hoppin' across the street and caught up with him."

"H'm," Jim said, frowning. He eyed Holloway oddly for a moment. "How'd you know who she was?"

"How?" Jake repeated. "She told me."

"Oh!"

"She told me she was lookin' for her husband an' that his name was Vance Kirby. Captain Vance Kirby, I shoulda said. Hey, I didn't know he used to be a captain in the cavalry."

"Looks like you know it now," Jim said dryly.

Holloway smiled thinly.

"Anyway," he went on, "she and Kirby talked for a minute, then he went on down the street, an' she hustled herself into Hanley's. She bought herself an outfit of dungarees an' stuff. She told Hanley she was goin' to California, an' said she wanted him to fix her up with everything she'd need. Hanley did what she wanted awright. He outfitted her with everything, right down to two horses, one for ridin', the other to pack her stuff on. I saw her come out of Hanley's, an' I wanna tell you, Jim, I never saw anything prettier-lookin' in dungarees in my life."

"Go on," Jim commanded. "I'm listenin'."

"There ain't much more to tell you. She picked Kirby up in front of Ed Jorgensen's lunchroom, and they pulled outta town an' headed westward. That's the story."

"H'm," Jim said again thoughtfully. "Did you tell that to John?"

Jake nodded gravely.

"To him an' to Jane, too," he replied. "Jim, we've been friends for a long time, an' I think as much of your kid as I do of anybody. So I don't wanna see her get hurt. Now if this Kirby has a wife already, what in blazes is Jane aimin' to be doin' about it? What was the idea of her ridin' off after him, 'specially after I told her about his wife bein' with him?"

Jim shook his head. "Not to give you a short answer, Jake," he said, "I'm damned if I know."

"Then that makes two of us. I couldn't figger it out either."

"Anybody else in town know about Mrs. Kirby?"

"Yeah, sure. Most everybody, I guess. You know how word gets around in a small town. And now it seems, everybody had it figgered out a long time ago that Jane an' Kirby were—well—sweet on each other. Don't ask me how they came to get that idea. All I can tell you is that they did. Sure looks like they had it right, doesn't it?"

Jim kept his thoughts to himself.

"There's just one thing more," Holloway said, and Jim

looked at him. "This afternoon young Lute Bailey rode into town loaded down for a long trip."

Jim's eyebrows arched in surprise.

"Full saddlebags, rifle in his saddle boot, cookin' things an' everything," Jake related. "I dunno what he found out about Kirby, but all of a sudden he went ridin' down the street like a bat outta hell. I saw him take the road leadin' outta town, but he kicked up so much dust he was plumb outta sight before I knew it."

"Lute was here earlier today."

"Oh, yeah? Did you tell him about Jane goin' off after Kirby?"

"Sure. He didn't come to see me. He came to see Jane. I had to tell him she wasn't here, an' I figgered he was entitled to know where she'd gone, so I told him."

"Uh-huh," Jake mused. 'Figgerin' that would tell him where he stood with Jane, an' that once he knew, he'd quit chasin' after her an' forget her. Was that the idea?"

"You might say so."

"But it didn't work out that way," Holloway said, and then he looked troubled. "I understand young Lute got madder'n all hell when he found out about Kirby goin' away with his wife. Lute insisted it musta been planned that way, that Kirby musta known his wife was comin' here to meet him. Anyway, Jim, he swore he'd kill Kirby. I dunno what good it'll do you to know that, but I got the idea that you oughta know it, an'—well—I've told you."

Jim nodded and sat back in his chair.

"I'm sure obliged to you, Jake," he said, "for going to so much trouble to get word to me. Look, how about a drink? Or maybe some coffee?"

Jake shook his head. "Don't want either one," he replied. He climbed stiffly to his feet, made a wry face and rubbed his right knee. "Gettin' old, awright. If I sit for more'n a couple o' minutes at a time, I get stiffer'n a board. Well, I'd better be gettin' back to town."

"Thanks again, Jake," Jim said, getting up from his chair.

"Forget it. If I hear anything else, Jim, I'll get word of it to you fast's I can."

"Swell."

They went to the door together. Jim stood in the doorway waiting for Holloway to climb up on his horse. It was

125

an effort for Jake, a futile one though, and finally, Jim had to come out of the house and give him a hand up.

"Made it!" Jake wheezed breathlessly, and Jim stepped back. Jake settled himself more securely in the saddle and got a firmer grip on the reins. "Doggone it, why in hell don't somebody get to breedin' horses that aren't so high an' so damned hard to get up on?"

"Dunno, Jake," Jim answered gravely. "But as a favour to you I'll look into it."

Holloway wheeled his mount.

"So long, Jim!" he yelled.

"So long, Jake!"

Holloway rode away into the night. Jim Whitaker closed the door and turned away from it slowly, carrying a new worry back with him to his chair.

"That blamed kid," he muttered as he seated himself again. "He's liable to do what he said he would. Leastways, he's liable to try to kill Kirby. Damn it all, anyway! Why don't the Baileys stay outta things once in a while an' give somebody else a chance?"

Then he thought of Jane, and he shook his head.

"Bet it was a helluva wallop to her when she heard about Kirby's wife bein' with him," he added, half aloud, and he shook his head again. "But why did she go on after hearin' that? What could she expect to gain by catchin' up with them? I wish to hell I'da gone with her instead o' lettin' John talk me out've it and lettin' him go. Doggone his hide!"

He got to his feet and started to pace the floor.

"There's always somethin' to worry about," he grumbled. "An' if it ain't one thing then it's another."

He stopped in his tracks and his head jerked up when he heard hoofbeats. He was rigid for a moment, listening. The frown on his face deepened. The clatter of hoofs swelled.

"Now what?" he demanded aloud. "Now who's bringin' me somethin' else to stew about?"

He stalked to the door and threw it open. A horseman rode around the house, and reined in.

"It's me, Jim," a voice called from the shadows beyond the doorway. "Gordon Bailey."

"Oh," Jim responded. "How are you?"

Bailey dismounted and Jim backed, holding the door for him. Gordon came into the house, hat in hand, and waited until Jim closed the door.

"Have a seat, Gordon," Jim invited, nodding in the direction of the table and the chairs around it. Bailey strode across the room, drew a chair away from the table, turned it around and sat down in it. Jim faced him, his hands in his pockets. "Awright, Gordon. What's botherin' you tonight? Lute?"

"Yes. I didn't realize he was so smitten with your daughter, Jim; that is, until just recently. He's gone after her. What's going to happen?"

"I dunno."

"I understand your brother John's gone with Jane. Is that right?"

Jim Whitaker nodded.

"Yes, and that's why I'm not worryin' too much 'bout how things are gonna come out," he replied. "Y'know, John's smart. He usually manages to find a way to handle things, and I know he'll figger a way outta this mess, too. Aside from the fact that he's been almost like a father to Jane, I know he likes Lute. I've heard him say so. So you can bet on it, Gordon, he isn't gonna stand by an' let either one of our kids get hurt. Leastways, not any more than he can help."

Gordon Bailey nodded.

"I'm glad to hear you say that," he said. "It's—well—it's conforting. Jim, do you think it would do any good if I were to go after them, too?"

Jim considered briefly, then he shook his head.

"Nope," he said flatly. "I don't think it'd do a bit o' good. Y'see, Gordon, they've got a heckuva head start on you. You'd have to ride like hell to catch up with them, an' for how long you'd have to keep goin' like all get-out—well—your guess is as good as mine. No, Gordon, you stay put. We'll leave things in John's hands an' hope for the best."

Gordon arose. He turned his hat over in his hands, ran his finger through the band, and then around the discoloured sweatband.

"Lute's all I've got, Jim," he said, raising his eyes to meet Jim's. The muscles in his jaws twitched for an instant. "Nothing else matters to me. If anything were to happen to him—"

"Nothing's gonna happen to him," Jim assured him. "The worst he can get outta this'll be a low-down feeling. But he's young, Gordon, and he'll get over it. And one fine day he'll meet another girl, an' believe me, that'll be that."

Gordon smiled wanly. "I hope you're right," he said.

His voice indicated that he wasn't fully convinced. However, he was willing to be, and his smile gave evidence of it. "Thanks, Jim, and good night."

"G'night, Gordon," Jim answered.

After Bailey had gone, Jim went back to his chair. He lounged in it for a while with his legs thrust out in front of him, his hands jammed deep in his pants pockets and a frown on his face. Then his head jerked up and the frown dissolved.

"How d'you like that?" he mused aloud. "I'm the one who needs a talkin' to because I'm worried sick, so instead o' someone comin' along an' givin' it to me, I gotta hand it out. Maybe I wasn't just talkin' through my hat. Maybe everything'll be all right. I sure hope so. I think I'm just gonna go on talkin' that into myself an' get started doin' things around here again so's I won't have time to think about th'm. And then all uva sudden Janey'll be back, and we'll go on living again like we used to. Yep, that's what I'm gonna do. If I don't I'll go loco."

He jerked his hands out of his pockets and got to his feet, squared his shoulders and went striding across the room to the cupboard. He bent over and opened the bottom drawer and took out his account books, pushed the drawer shut with his foot, carried the books to the table and opened them. He fished in his pocket for his pencil, produced it, eyed the blunted lead point a bit doubtfully, shrugged his shoulders and drew his chair closer.

CHAPTER EIGHTEEN

THERE was an uncomfortable and penetrating chill in the early morning air, and Diane, huddling in her jacket, with her chin buried in the depths of her upturned collar and her hands jammed deep in her pockets, moved closer to the fire over which Kirby was frying some bacon. Behind them, the tied-up horses, eager to be on the move again, milled about, pawed the ground impatiently and tugged on their tethering lines. Diane glanced in their direction and frowned; when she turned her head again and found Kirby's eyes on her, she flushed.

"They can be awf'lly annoying at times," she said defensively. Then she added quickly, "It's cold, isn't it? Goes right through me."

"It'll warm up presently," Kirby answered. He looked skyward for a moment. "Probably before we get started."

She dug her hands deeper into her pockets, but they were too shallow to give her much comfort.

"Aren't there any towns between here and California?" she asked.

"A couple. Why?"

"I was just thinking how wonderful it would be," she said, and she added hastily, "just for a night, you know, to sleep in a real warm bed and eat a regular meal sitting at a table. Wouldn't it be luxurious?"

"Yes," he admitted. "I guess it would."

This was the first time she had even intimated that she missed the comforts and the luxuries to which she had always been accustomed. The mountains were still hundreds of miles away, but he thought of them now because eventually they would have to cross them. If the cold bothered her now, what would she do when they ran into snow and sleet and icy winds whipped about them and buffeted them unmercifully?

"When we come to a town, can't we spend the night there in a hotel?" she asked. "We could be up and on our way again as early the next morning as you wanted."

"Yes, I suppose so. We'll have to be watching for a town pretty soon now. Our supplies are beginning to thin out. Y'see, I didn't buy much of anything. No point in loading ourselves down until we have to."

"Oh," she said.

He averted his eyes then, busying himself with the bacon. He looked up again shortly.

"Sit on that rock, Diane," he said, pointing to a flat rock close by the fire. "The grass is still too damp."

She eyed the rock somewhat doubtfully.

"It looks cold," she said shortly.

"I think you'll find it anything but cold," he said quietly. "The fire must have warmed it up."

She bent down, touched it gingerly and smiled up at him over her hunched shoulder.

"It is warm," she said and seated herself on it. "Wonderfully warm."

He grunted, filled a plate with bacon and handed it to her; when she was able to handle it, he brought her a cup of steaming hot coffee. Then with a plate of bacon in one hand and a cup in the other hand, he squatted down on the ground, cross-legged, on the opposite side of the fire. They ate in silence. She was finished before he was even half-way through. He looked at her.

"Want s'more?" he asked. "Some more coffee?"

"Nothing more, thank you," she replied, wiping her finger tips on the grass at her feet. "Vance, what are you planning to do when we get to California?"

"I'd like to get a small place of my own."

"Won't that take money? A lot of it, I mean?"

"I don't know. If it does, then I'll have to forget the idea and go to work at whatever I can get."

"I see," she said slowly. She was silent for a moment, even looked away for an instant, then she turned to him again. "Vance . . ."

"Yes?"

"Have you ever thought of Canada?" she asked. "I wonder if there wouldn't be even greater opportunity for you there? A new, rich, vast country with unlimited natural resources. At least, that's what I've been told."

He drained his cup and put it down.

"Think you'd like Canada better than California?"

She smiled at him.

"I don't really know anything about either of them other than what I've been told," she replied. "So I can't say which I'd prefer. However, I think Canada might be worth considering."

"All right. We don't have to make a decision right away, do we?"

"No, of course not," she said quickly. "However, I'll like it anywhere as long as we're there together."

He climbed to his feet, stamped out the fire; he stopped abruptly and looked down at her.

"Maybe I shouldn't have done that so soon," he said. "Are you any warmer now?"

"Oh, yes!" she said. "Lots warmer."

As proof of it she pushed down her collar and even opened her jacket. He took care of the plates and the cups, the frying pan and finally the coffeepot, cleansed them and stowed them away in his saddlebags. As she arose, he trudged away to the brush, untied the horses and brought them forward, strapped on Diane's bedroll and his blankets, hoisted the trunk to the pack horse's back and lashed it on, then he turned to Diane.

"All right," he said.

She came to him at once. He helped her mount her

horse. When she was settled in the saddle, he handed her the reins and started away towards his own horse.

"Vance!"

He halted and looked at her questioningly.

"Please," she said.

He retraced his steps to her side and looked up at her.

"You weren't very glad to see me the other morning," she said with a smile. "Do you feel any differently now?"

Their eyes met and held.

"I don't know, Diane," he answered. "A lot of things have happened to me since I saw you last, and I've held you responsible for some of them. But, in time, I suppose I'll forget them. That is, the part you played in them."

He turned on his heel and marched over to his horse and reached for the reins. He stopped and turned his head and looked at her again.

"But it will take time," he concluded. He swung himself up into the saddle. "All right, Diane?"

"Yes," she said. "All right."

Kirby nudged his mount with his knees, and the animal stirred into movement. Kirby rode in the lead, with Diane just slightly behind him and the pack horse bringing up the rear. Light suddenly flooded the horizon, and the range was instantly ablaze with bright, warm, cheerful sunshine. Kirby twisted around to Diane, who smiled again and nodded.

"Wonderful," she said. "Isn't it?"

Kirby settled himself again; he quickened the pace and the other two horses followed his lead. Miles and miles of open range country fell away behind them. Then there was a tiny, curling wisp of smoke somewhere ahead of them, and Diane, sitting upright astride her horse, watched it interestedly, held by it, watched it climb skyward lazily and gently and finally dissolve into nothingness.

Fifteen or twenty minutes later they came to the lip of a tiny green valley, and they drew rein and looked down. Below them was a small ranch. In the middle of it was a rambling ranch house, painted green and white with smoke from its stack lifting into the morning sky. Beyond the house was a red barn, then a shack of some sort, probably a tool shed, and a corral. There were a couple of horses in the corral, and they wheeled around the confines of the enclosure happily. A dog appeared, coming from the direction of the barn, and he dashed around the corral barking loudly and pursuing the cavorting horses. When they paid no attention to him, he ran in under the bars that formed the enclosure; when the horses swerved towards him, he fled for his life, raced around the barn and disappeared behind it.

Then they saw a woman emerge from the barn; there was a cry from within it and she stopped and turned. A child ran out, and the woman laughed and held out her arms; the child ran into them. Beyond the barn was a clothesline, and the wash on it whipped about in the morning breeze. A man appeared, coming into the scene from the rear of the house. He called and waved, and the child broke away from its mother and ran to him. Kirby stole a look at Diane. There was a smile on her half-parted lips.

They wheeled away from the valley. They rode on at a fairly steady pace, and again the range miles slipped away behind them. At noon, when the sun was almost directly overhead, they halted for something to eat. As before, it was Kirby who prepared their meal of hot cakes and coffee; when they were finished, he gathered the things together and washed them with water from his canteen; while he was so engaged, Diane arose from the rock on which she had been sitting and strolled off. He found her, minutes later, standing on a rise that commanded a view of the open countryside. She did not appear to hear his step as he came towards her.

"Ready, Diane?" he asked, halting just below her.

She jerked suddenly and flushed.

"Ready," she answered.

He turned away from her. She started down the tiny slope, lost her footing on the grass and slid. She screamed, and he wheeled and lunged for her, caught her in his arms and steadied her. When she looked up at him and smiled, he led her down the rest of the way to level ground.

"Wait here," he told her.

He marched off, returning a moment later with her horse. He helped her climb up and handed her the reins. She smiled her thanks, but he turned away without a response and tramped back to his own horse. When he rode forward with the pack horse following him, she wheeled into position behind him, shooing the pack horse away. The trunk-laden animal ranged forward alongside of Kirby, who merely glanced at him.

The early afternoon, midafternoon and late afternoon hours wore away. Then in the distance, probably a mile ahead of them, a town loomed up. Kirby turned and motioned to Diane, and she rode up alongside him and followed his pointing finger with her eyes.

"Oh!" she said. "A town! At last!"

They clattered townward at a quickened pace, with the trunk thumping up and down on the back of the pack horse and threatening to break its bonds and disgorge Diane's personal possessions in a wildly scattered array. Kirby shot a questioning glance at it a couple of times and even wheeled alongside the pack horse for a closer view of the galloping animal's burden. He checked their pace, slowed it to a mere trot, and finally, to a walk when they rode down a dirt incline and on to a street that was the town. It was the shortest street he had ever seen, and by the same token, the smallest town. Actually it was hardly more than a stagecoach station, or a settlement, for the town consisted of the street and a dozen buildings with the largest, a two-storey-high structure, in the middle of them. A tattered, wind-torn canvas sign atop the building read "Hotel", and they wheeled towards it.

"Do you think they'll have a bathtub, Vance?" Diane asked eagerly.

Kirby shrugged his shoulders.

"I don't know," he answered, his eyes ranging over the street ahead of them. "But if they don't, we'll rig up something for you that'll be just as serviceable."

There was a general store, and a man with an apron around his ample middle came out and looked at them. They pulled up in front of the hotel, and Kirby dismounted. He helped Diane to the ground, and she followed him into the hotel. There was a small lobby, a small desk, a row of wooden slots on the wall behind the desk for the guests' mail. Just beyond the desk was a stairway that led to the upper floor. There was a slow, tired step, and a pock-marked man, with shiny silver-rimmed spectacles half-way down the bridge of his nose, appeared and greeted them with a stare.

"Rooms are two bucks a day," he announced without any preliminaries. "In advance."

"All right," Kirby said.

"Two an' a half with a bath."

"With a bath," Kirby said, producing the money.

"Right," the hotelkeeper said, taking the money and putting it in his pants pocket. "Room two-o-two. Water pitcher's in the bathroom. Lemme know when you're ready, an' I'll show you where to draw your water."

"What about our horses?" Kirby wanted to know.

"We only allow two-legged critters in here," the man said with a grin that revealed yellowish teeth. He laid his gaze on Diane now and seemed to enjoy what he saw, for his eyes appeared to open a bit wider. Suddenly he jerked his head, and he looked at Kirby again, appraisingly. "There's a stable down the street. You can tell where it is by standin' right outside for a minute, raisin' your head an' sniffin' once good an' hard. Feller named Oates runs it, an' that's no joke cause that's his name. Leastways, he says it is. Anyway, Mister, you tell Oates we sent you, an' he'll charge half the regular rate."

"Vance," Diane said, and Kirby glanced at her over his shoulder. "Do you think it would be too much trouble for you to get my trunk?"

"I'll bring it upstairs for you," he replied. "Come on. We'll have a look at the room first, then I'll get the trunk."

"Here y'are," the man said. He handed Kirby a key. He nodded in the direction of the stairway, watched them mount the stairs, then he called, "If anything ain't just right, holler, an' I'll come a-runnin'."

"That I should like to see," Diane whispered to Kirby. "He doesn't look like the kind who could run more than a step without falling flat on his face."

The street was dark and shadowy, for it was almost ten o'clock; save for the hotel and the saloon at the far corner the town had closed for the night. Kirby was idling in front of the hotel when he heard the approach of crunching wheels. He raised his eyes. A buckboard came down the incline, its wheels grinding and spinning dirt; then it was in the street. He watched it approach and brake to a rasping stop directly in front of him. Two men climbed down from it. One of them was tall and rangy, and he wore a low-slung gun with its open-ended holster tied down around his right thigh; his companion was older, shorter and stocky, and his manner and attire marked him as city-bred. They halted on the narrow wooden sidewalk and looked up at the hotel. They glanced at Kirby; then with the tall man leading the way, they stalked past him and into the lobby. Kirby turned his head and followed them with his eyes. They stopped at the desk, and the tall man banged on it with his fist. There was a moment's wait, but then the pock-marked hotel-keeper appeared and talked with them in a voice that suddenly became low-pitched and guarded. Kirby was disappointed because he couldn't hear what was being said.

When he heard a step coming towards him, he turned his head away quickly and looked skyward. The man with the low-slung gun sauntered out and stopped beside him, but Kirby pretended to be too absorbed in his study of the moon and the stars and the sky itself to notice him.

"Excuse me, partner," the tall man drawled, and Kirby looked at him.

"Oh," he said, pretending to be surprised.

The man smiled thinly.

"Your name Kirby?" he asked. "Vance Kirby?"

Instantly Kirby sensed that he had made a mistake in giving the hotel-keeper his right name. He cursed himself inwardly for having been so stupid, realizing all too late that he should have used an assumed name.

"Who are you?" he asked.

"Name's Walker." The man flipped back his coat. A silver badge that was pinned to his suspenders gleamed brightly at Kirby, whose heart sank. Everything was over for him, he told himself bitterly. But then it didn't matter. Nothing mattered any longer.

"All right," he said. "I'm Kirby. What d'you want of me?"

"Don't want anything o' you 'cept some information," was the quiet reply.

Kirby's eyebrows arched, but he controlled himself.

"Information?" he repeated. "What about?"

"You're registered here with a Mrs. Kirby."

"What about it?"

"I'm takin' it for granted she's your wife."

Kirby's eyes glinted. "She is," he said curtly.

His hands dropped. The marshal's eyes followed them; when they stopped and the thumbs hooked themselves in Kirby's gun belt, he looked up again.

"Got a picture of 'er maybe? On you, I mean."

"No."

The marshal's hand dipped into his coat pocket; he drew out something and held it up for Kirby to see.

"This her?" he asked. "Look anything like her?"

Kirby's eyes shifted from the man's face to the thing he was holding up. It was a photograph of Diane. There was something handwritten across the bottom of it.

"This her?" the marshal asked a second time.

"Looks like her," Kirby answered calmly.

"Uh-huh. How 'bout the handwriting? Recognize it?"

Kirby glanced at it.

"It could be hers," he answered.

"C'n you read it?"

Kirby took the photograph in his hands. It was Diane. There was no question about it. He turned so that the lamplight from the lobby lit up the face in the photograph. It made the writing readable too.

" 'With all my love, Diane,' " he read aloud, grunted and handed it back.

"That her name, Diane?"

"Yes."

The marshal returned the photograph to his coat pocket.

"She hasn't been your wife, partner, for a month o' Sundays," he said simply. "She got a divorce from you in Kansas City an' married a feller named Corning. That's him inside. Wanna meet him?"

"Not particularly."

The marshal shrugged.

"Suit yourself," he said. "You interested in knowin' why we're after your wife? Leastways, the woman you thought was still your wife?"

"I'm curious."

"Awright," the lawman said. "Corning's a banker. Seems he met up with the lady an' liked her right off. She let him know she felt the same way about him; then she told him 'bout bein' married to you. She told she'd have divorced you long before, only she couldn't finance the deal. He put up the dough for her after she promised to marry him the minute she was free. She did just that. Got herself unhitched from you and married Corning."

"Very interesting."

"Maybe, but that ain't everything she did. The lady, Mrs. Corning, if you don't mind, partner . . ."

"I don't mind in the least."

The marshal grinned at Kirby.

"Thanks," he said. "Anyway, the lady dipped into the strong box of Corning's bank and cleaned it out. If it had been just Corning's dough that she took that would have been awright, leastways with the law. It woulda been up to Corning to get it back from her, or as much as she was willing to give back. But it happened that a good-sized piece o' that dough belonged to the United States Government and so did the bonds she took with her when she hightailed it. Now the government's hollerin' for its dough and the bonds, too. And it wants Mrs. Corning for stealin' th'm. That's the story, partner."

"Thanks for telling it to me," Kirby said. "But believe it or not, Marshal, I didn't know anything about those things: the divorce, Corning, the money and so on."

"I know you didn't," the marshal answered. "You couldn't have, 'less of course she told you, an' I knew doggoned well she wouldn't do that an' spoil things for herself. We've been trailin' her for quite a spell now, an' we know you weren't with her till she joined up with you in some one-horse town a couple o' hundred miles east of here. So you're in the clear, Kirby. Where is she? Upstairs?"

"Yes."

"You wanna see her? I mean, before we take her away?"

Kirby thought about it briefly, then he shook his head.

"No," he said with finality. "I don't want to see her. She isn't my responsibility any longer. She's Corning's wife and therefore his responsibility."

The marshal grinned again.

"I'm glad to hear you say that," he said. "For a while there I was afraid you might get some fool idea in your head about tryin' to do somethin' for her. You know. To help her get away from me just to give her a chance even though she doesn't deserve it," the marshal continued.

"I'm finished with her," Kirby said.

"Uh-huh. Then suppose you go somewheres?" the marshal suggested. "I know you don't wanna make it any harder on 'er than it is already. It'll be a lot easier on her, if you aren't around when we bring her downstairs. What d'you say, partner?"

"Right. I'm going."

The marshal stepped back. Kirby strode away. The marshal waited; when he saw Kirby reach the corner and turn into the saloon, he marched back into the hotel.

CHAPTER NINETEEN

SINCE early morning Kirby had had the feeling that he was being trailed. He had felt it first when he was breaking camp, and the feeling that he was being watched had per-

137

sisted throughout the long morning. But he had given no outward or betraying indication of his suspicion, and he had ridden on doggedly, never once turning to look back in hopes of catching even the briefest glimpse of his pursuer. Grimly too he had held his horse to the same even pace, checking him sharply the instant he showed impatience, and an inclination to lengthen his stride. The level range-land with its far-spreading rumpled carpet of green and brown had been supplanted by rough, hilly terrain, and the westward trail that he was following wound uphill and downhill in turn, through ravines and defiles and slate-coloured canyons, whose sheer walls rang and echoed to the metallic beat of his horse's hoofs.

Ordinarily, the faintest suspicion that he was being trailed would have resulted in the adoption of prompt protective measures. He would have scurried for cover and then, crouching behind a tree stump or a boulder, with his gun in his hand, raised and ready for a quick shot, he would have awaited the appearance of the man who was dogging his trail. Or he would have swung off the trail and circled back in an effort to outflank and come up behind the man. But he did nothing. It mattered little what happened to him. He had almost no interest what-soever in his pursuer or in knowing who the man was or the purpose of his pursuit. Life, he told himself bitterly, held nothing for him. He would always be a wanted and hunted man. The marshal, he had already decided, hadn't known anything about him or he wouldn't have let him go. Soon, though, another law officer would pick him up, and that would be the end of everything.

Of course, the farther west he got, the less chance there was of his being apprehended. But he would never be able to take root anywhere and grow, because the fear of hav-ing a pursuer come upon him suddenly would always be present.

He was glad he was alone again, glad that Diane was gone, although he was sorry for her. But he didn't intend to be hypocritical about her. She meant very little to him. Given a brief span of time, he was sure the memory of her would fade away until he would be hard put to really recall her. Of course it would never be that way where Jane was concerned. He would never forget her.

Now he was getting impatient. Why didn't his pursuer overtake him? Hadn't he given him every opportunity? What was the matter with the fellow? His mouth tightened.

Presently he'd be through the canyon, and then he would force the issue to a conclusion. He would halt and wait for the man to come up to him. . . . Suddenly he realized that he hadn't heard the hoofbeats behind him for some time, and he began to wonder what had happened. Did it mean that his pursuer had abandoned the pursuit? He couldn't understand it, and it irked him. Well, regardless, he'd stop when he emerged from the canyon.

Presently he was riding onto a widening trail. There was level ground ahead, and he could see grass, too. There were just a couple of huge, white-faced boulders to be passed, and he'd be in the open again. He looked skyward. There were fleecy clouds overhead. They weren't real clouds; they were just puffs of white that hung gently in the vast expanse of sky. The air was warm and clear, and there was a breath of flowers in it. It was a day for living, and here he was offering someone an opportunity to kill him. Then his horse stopped abruptly, so suddenly that he was jolted forward in the saddle, and he frowned and raised his eyes again. Standing atop a boulder with the barrel of his levelled gun shining in the bright sunlight was a man. It was Lute Bailey. They looked at each other. No greeting, not even the briefest of curt nods, not even the barest sign of recognition passed between them. The muzzle of Lute's gun gaped hungrily and menacingly at Kirby.

"Get your hands up," the youth commanded.

Kirby did not move.

"Get your hands up," the youth repeated, louder this time.

When Kirby did not move, Lute scowled darkly.

"Awright," he said curtly. "Don't hafta. But don't try any tricks. Y'hear?"

There was no response from Kirby. He continued to sit quietly and motionlessly and Lute, a little flustered, eyed him a moment longer. Then he eased himself down the side of the boulder, came up behind Kirby, reached up and jerked Kirby's gun out of its holster and promptly backed away. Around Kirby's horse he moved and, when he was facing Kirby again, he stopped.

"I'm takin' you back with me," he announced. "I'm gonna give the law a chance to give you what's comin' to you."

He waited, but there was no response from Kirby. His attitude evidently puzzled the youth, for he frowned even

139

more darkly than before, and he glared at the silent and motionless man.

"I know the law's anxious to get its hooks into you," Lute went on again presently. "I know because you told me. Never thought I'd use that against you, did you, huh? Well, I am, and I'm gonna see you swing. Then I won't ever hafta worry about you again or about Jane either. You'll be outta the way and outta her life for good."

Kirby's horse whinnied and pawed the ground impatiently, and Lute took his eyes off Kirby for a moment to glare at the animal; then he raised them again to Kirby.

"What'd you do with your wife?" Lute demanded. "Ditch her somewheres along the way so's you could make room for Jane?"

Kirby was still mute, and Lute began to show his annoyance. His hand tightened around the butt of his gun.

"I oughta kill you right here an' now," he said through his teeth. "You'd like me to do that. Beats dyin' at the end of a rope a dozen different ways from the ace, don't it? But I won't kill you. No. That'd be makin' things too easy for you. Besides, I'd only be cheatin' myself outta somethin' I'm lookin' forward to. Seein' you dangle at the end of a rope."

"You'd better kill me while you've got the chance," Kirby said quietly.

"Yeah?" Lute said tauntingly.

"Yes, because I'm not going back with you or with anyone else."

"Oh, you're not, huh?"

"No."

Lute came striding up to the horse. He grabbed the reins and pulled, but the horse did not move.

"Move, damn you!" Lute yelled at the horse. "Turn around!"

He dropped the reins and swung wildly at the horse; the animal hastily shied away and reared up, wheeling with its hoofs pawing the air above Lute's head. The startled youth hurriedly backed against a boulder, crouching a bit, with his eyes wide and his mouth open. Kirby jerked the reins and spoke sharply, and the horse came down again on all fours. Lute came erect again. He was white-faced.

"Turn around," he commanded, gesturing with his gun.

Kirby shook his head.

"I'm gonna give you one last chance to do what I tell

you," Lute said angrily, patches of red dancing up into his cheeks. "I'm gonna count to three, an' if you don't turn around I'm gonna kill you. An' I'm not foolin'. Y'hear? Awright now. One—two—three!"

There was no movement on Kirby's part. His horse pawed the ground again. Lute's gun roared thunderously, and a bullet ploughed the earth directly between the horse's feet and showered the animal with dirt. A second bullet, fired into just about the same spot, produced about the same result. The horse snorted protestingly when dirt spewed over his legs. The gun came down for a third shot, but it was never fired: instead it dropped in Lute's hand to his side and with a jerky movement up and into his holster. He snatched Kirby's gun out of his belt and sent it slithering over the rough ground. It collided with the horse's hoof, and the animal looked down at it curiously.

"Y'knew I couldn't do it!" the youth cried, raging in front of Kirby. "Y'knew it all along but because you wanted to make a fool outta me, you let me go ahead. There's your gun. Get down an' get it an' shoot me. I won't try to stop you. Go on, damn you! Go on!"

Then there were hoofbeats behind them, and they turned and looked back wonderingly. Two horsemen— no, one of them was a girl—came spurring along the canyon path. The girl lashed her mount, and bounded ahead of her companion. It was Jane, and she came up to them in a dust-raising slide. She flung herself off her horse, ran forward a bit and faltered to an awkward, hesitant stop, her eyes shuttling from Kirby to Lute, then up to Kirby again. Her companion came clattering up. It was Uncle John. No one saw him dismount or paid any attention to him because all eyes were on Jane. Kirby swung himself off his horse, and Jane ran to him.

"Oh, Vance!" she cried. "I was afraid we'd never find you! Are you—are you all right? Those shots we heard— we were afraid something had happened to you."

Her anxious eyes probed his face, while her hands gripped his arms.

"We met Diane," she went on a bit breathlessly, and Lute stared at her. "We stopped overnight at a small-town hotel, and she was there. The men who were taking her away—well, they were having some difficulty with her and, when we heard the commotion, I offered to do what I could to help quiet her. She was hysterical. They let me

141

in to talk with her. Actually it worked out the other way around. She wanted to talk, so I let her. She talked excitedly at first, even incoherently, but she calmed down as she went on, and she told me everything, quite rationally too. You're a free man, Vance. You're as free as the air."

There was bewilderment in his eyes. Lute's jaw hung a bit as his eyes shifted from one to the other, trying desperately but evidently unsuccessfully to understand what Jane was talking about.

"Free?" he heard Kirby repeat, and he stared at him again. "Free?" Kirby said hollowly. "Free of her, yes, but not of those other things that have been hanging over my head all this time. I'll never be free of them as long as I live."

"You don't understand!" Jane cried. She turned, and John Whitaker moved to her side. He thrust out his right hand to Kirby, who stared at him blankly. John laughed and grabbed Kirby's hand and pumped it up and down vigorously. "Uncle John," Jane pleaded. "You tell him, please."

"Sure, honey," he said. He looked into Kirby's face. "What Jane's tryin' to tell you, Son, is that that woman, that Diane, told the marshal whatever his name was . . ."

"Walker," Jane said at once.

"Uh-huh, Walker. Well, it seems she told the marshal that you plugged that Trevvett feller but that you didn't kill him. As a matter o' fact, he's alive today. Leastways, he was the last time she heard of him, and from what she heard he was cuttin' up same as usual so he had to be in pretty good shape to do that. Then that feller you plugged when you were makin' your getaway. Seems he was wanted by the law, an' there was a price on his head. So by killin' him you did the law a great big favour. Saved it the cost o' bringin' him to trial an' keepin' him eatin' while he was in prison, which is where he woulda wound up if it hadn't been for you. The way it stands now, nobody's lookin' for you an' nobody wants you . . ."

"I do," Jane said, smiling up at Kirby.

John looked at her and at Kirby. He coughed behind his hand and backed a bit, collided with Lute, took him by the arm and led him away, despite the youth's reluctance to leave the scene.

The tensed and bewildered expression was beginning to lift from Kirby's face, an indication that he was beginning to understand a lot of things. Jane did not press him. She wanted things to clarify themselves for him without further explanation from her. Then a new light came into his eyes, a brightness that she had never seen in them before. She watched him, and her heart sang.

"You mean I can even go back into the service?" he asked eagerly after another moment.

"If you like," she answered. "And you would like that, wouldn't you?"

He nodded and smiled. "If they'd take me back," he said.

"The marshal said he'd be sending his report to Washington within a day or two," she related. "He suggested that you wait a week before submitting your request for reinstatement so that the authorities would have his report before your application came up for consideration. He said he wouldn't be at all surprised if you were ordered to report to your old regiment within a month's time. Oh, yes, Vance! Here's something else that I nearly forgot to mention. He said something about a Major Hunter—"

"Colonel Hunter," Kirby corrected. "He was my regimental commander."

"Oh," she said. "Well, Major or Colonel, the marshal said he knows him, and he's sending him a copy of his report and a personal letter. So Captain Kirby—"

He stiffened to attention.

"Your orders, Madam?" he asked gravely.

She thought about it for a moment.

"First, Captain Kirby," she said equally grave. "You've treated me shamefully. I've come more than three hundred miles to find you, and you haven't even rewarded me with a polite 'thank you.' Second, you've—"

He caught her in his arms and held her tight. He kissed her hungrily.

"First, second, third," he said when he released her for a moment, "and all the way up to a million, I love you. We're heading eastward at once, and the minute we find someone who's authorized to perform a wedding ceremony, you'll be Mrs. Vance Kirby. Then we'll get that application for reinstatement off to Washington. And after a while we'll get started for Arizona. We'd better let the War Department know that we can be reached at the old fort so we won't be losing a minute's time reporting for duty."

"Goodness," she said. "You certainly do move swiftly when you go into action. Don't you?"

They looked at each other in surprise when they turned to speak to Uncle John and found he had gone. But then there was a hail from the canyon trail, and they turned in its direction quickly. Two horsemen were idling there, waiting for them, and one of them, John Whitaker, was beckoning them.

Kirby kissed her again, and she clung to him. But after the second hail she stirred in his arms.

"They're waiting for us," she whispered.

"Let 'em wait," he answered. "We've waited longer."

It was only when his impatient horse whinnied, and failing to get a response from Kirby, came up behind them and nudged them with his head that Kirby was willing to release her. He led her to her horse and lifted her into the saddle and handed her the reins, then he went back to his own horse and swung up astride him. He rode forward to her side.

"Ready?" he asked.

She tightened her grip on the reins and settled herself a bit more comfortably in the saddle.

"Ready," she answered brightly.

Together they rode through the canyon. The slate walls rang with the echoing clatter of their horses' hoofs. Ahead of them the waiting horsemen wheeled their mounts, waved and rode away. Kirby reached out and Jane gave him her free hand. Presently they emerged from the canyon and swung onto the trail that led eastward.

THE END